A Love Worth the Fight

3

D1249629

By

Nona Day

Natavia Presents

Is now accepting submissions!
Genres accepted range from Urban
Fiction, African American
Romance, Interracial Romance,
Street Lit, Paranormal Fiction,
and more...

Please send:

1. First Five Chapters
2. Synopsis
3. Contact information
to Natavia.stewart@yahoo.com

Fila

"Call this number. Since he doesn't recognize your number, he's not going to say anything when he answers. Just tell him who you are, and I need a lawyer ASAP," I told Pops over the jailhouse phone. I was using my one call to get in touch with Dose. I know he's in Jamaica with Sheba. I'm hoping he could use his connections to get me the fuck outta here. I know I fucked up letting Estelle and her trifling mama get in my head. She knew when it came to Fiji I would lose my damn mind. There was no way I was leaving my son there, so they could poison his head with negative shit about me. The bad part is they still have him, and I'm locked the fuck up. Fiji has never seen me mad. I can't imagine what's going through his little mind right now. He watched me hit his grandma, and nearly beat his uncle to death. At this point I hope the bitch nigga die.

"I gotcha Son," Pops said before ending the call. The guard escorted me back to the jail cell. I wasn't planning on being here for long. I've been hustling since I was fifteen. This is the first time I've been locked up. It's funny when I think about it. I was always concerned about being locked up for hustling. Here I am locked up for whooping a nigga's ass. I started thinking about Paisley. I can't believe she went on a date with that bitch nigga. I guess she was serious when she said she wanted to slow things down between us. I understood her frustration with the mess I had with Estelle. I never thought she would be out here trying to fuck another nigga. I guess it was some truth to what Tanika said. I'm going to fall back from all the bullshit, focus on making money and getting my son from that crazy ass family.

I was in the holding cell with a bunch of niggas waiting to be put in a cell for our stay here. I knew I would be staying the night. I'm hoping I'll be out of here first thing in the morning. I looked around the cell at all the young cats that looked comfortable being locked in a cage. This shit wasn't for me. I showed a poker face for everyone to see, but I was on edge on the inside. It wasn't fear that I was feeling. It was the thought of having my freedom taken away. I didn't want to be told when to eat, piss and shit. I didn't want to be identified by a number. My parents named me Frederick Antonio McCormick. The streets named me Fila. I got the nick name because I loved rocking the old school tennis shoes. I have them custom made to fit the outfit I wore each day.

"Yo, you used to roll with Majesty. Where that fuck nigga at? He got my damn sister pregnant, and jetted," the dark skin slender guy said mean mugging me. I didn't reply to his comment. A few other niggas started looking at me as if they had some kind of beef with me.

"Don't you hear my boy talking to you?" A big fat ass nigga said walking up to me.

I smirked. "If you know I heard him. You should know I was ignoring his question. Now, get the fuck out my face." I had already prepared myself to body this big nigga.

"Mothafucka you might run the streets, but you don't run shit in here," he said stepping in closer to me. When a nigga can't get on your level they try to bring you down to theirs. I had a choice I could walk away or whoop his big ass to let him know I'm not the bitch in the dog pound. I gave him a hard blow to the right side of his mouth. He stumbled backwards. All the other inmates formed a circle around us. He lend forward, charged me and grabbed me around the waist. He was trying to pick me up to slam me to the floor. I raised my arms and came down on his back with both my elbows as hard as I could. I felt his grip loosen, but he was still holding on trying to throw me. I came down on his back again. He let go and swung at me. He never came close to my face as I dodged his lick. I gave him to more quick jabs to the face causing blood to spew from his mouth. He was no fighter. Every punch he threw, I dodged. I would follow up with a combination to his face and body. We fought until he got tired and fell to the floor. The next thing I knew, I was being jumped by a gang of niggas. I fought off as many as I could until they got the best of me. Two held my arms while another one was hitting me in the face and stomach. I used the two holding me as a brace to lift my body up. I lifted my body and kicked the dude hitting me in the face. He fell down holding his nose. I knew the shit was broke. The two guys let me go causing me to fall to the floor. I jumped up as quick as they dropped me. I was ready to take any nigga in here who thought I was a nigga to fuck with.

"McCormick! Break that shit up! You gotta visitor," the guard said walking up to the cell. I knew Dose would come through. I just never thought he would be this fast. The guard handcuffed me before letting me out the cell. After letting me out, he escorted me into a small room that had only a table, and two chairs. I sat across from the middle aged white man that was dressed in a cheap suit. I don't know who the fuck he was, but I know Dose didn't send him. I stared at him when he finally looked up at me. I knew this wasn't going to go well.

"I want a lawyer," I demanded staring at him.

He smirked. "First, let me introduce myself. My name is Detective Bailey. I see you have some pretty heavy charges, attempted kidnapping and murder."

"I can't kidnap my own damn son, and whooping a man's ass doesn't equate to murder," I told him.

"They don't expect him to make it. If he dies, you will be charged with murder. If you work with me, I will work with you," he tried bribing me.

I laughed. "I need to talk with my lawyer." I don't know what the fuck he wanted from me, and I didn't plan on sitting here listening.

"I will bury you. I've discovered a lot of information about you in a short period of time. I'm curious as to how you were able to open so many businesses. You have never worked. It's in your best interest to take my offer," he warned me. This is why I stayed low key . I didn't want these crooked mothafuckas in my pockets. I already knew where this was going. I'm sure he was looking to get paid to keep quiet about my illegal dealings.

"Like I said I want to talk to my lawyer," I repeated staring him in the eyes.

He stood up and stared down at me. "You dumb nigga. I will make sure you never see your son again," he said in a low voice before walking out the room.

Basilio

Moreno and I sat there staring at each other. Neither of us said a word or moved a muscle. The two guards stood over me pointing their weapons at my head. I know Moreno wanted to kill me, but he couldn't. I was more valuable to him alive than dead. He had already loss major profits with Sanchez's dead body laying in front of us. There were only three members of his family left. Hector didn't have the mindset to make the money I could. Chiraq would continue to bring him major profits. Moreno would still be taking a major loss with me and Sanchez dead. Moreno seen it before the guards did. The red dots rested on both the guard's third eye. Moreno eyes grew wide as I smirked. The two guard's bodies dropped to the floor with a hole in their domes. I may have walked in the building alone, but I wasn't stupid. Guap had his team posted outside. The many windows allowed them to have a clear shot.

"Looks like it's just me and you," I said with a smile.

"You are playing a dangerous game," he said staring at me with a blank face.

A Love Worth the Fight 3   Nona Day

"I'm playing your game. I want my family to walk away. Your rule is there must be a blood sacrifice. I'm sacrificing myself," I reminded him.

"You are half right Bull. It's my game and my rules. You don't get to decide you will be sacrificed. That's my choice," he said with a smirk. I launched toward him. I jacked him up by his shirt ready to body him, but I knew I couldn't. Moreno was the only one that could assure my family's safety. I needed him alive. We were more valuable to each other alive than dead.

"Calm down Bull. You know I'm a fair man. You can still save your family." I don't care what I had to do. I will do whatever to make sure everyone walks away alive and free.

"You know when my father died I wasn't prepared to take over in his place. I was living a carefree life. Honestly, I miss that life. I had to step up and be the man he raised me to be. You can understand that can't you?" He asked. I didn't reply.

"Let's have a seat, and discuss the dilemma we've found ourselves in," he said trying to charm me. I couldn't understand Moreno. This wasn't the man I've known him to be. He has always been the one to negotiate. For once, it's his way or no way. I let him go, and we both took a seat.

"You know what I want. I want out with my family's freedom and safety," I reminded him.

"And what's in it for me. You have killed Anthony and Sanchez. Eduardo is dead. With you gone I'm left with Hector and Chiraq. I know Chiraq is valuable, but he's in Jamaica making his profits. Hector can't do what you and Sanchez do for my pockets. I can't let you walk away nor can I kill you."

"I don't give a fuck what you do to me. My family is my only concern. I know you hold their fate in your hands." Moreno was a part of a cartel. He would have to get their approval to let my family leave.

"What will I have to offer them for your family's safety if you are dead?" He asked. "They won't let Dose be head of the family because he is not your family's blood."

"I don't want to kill you Bull. You are too valuable to me, and you know this. I could give you Sanchez's territory and it would be just like he was never a part of the family. You would bring in more money than he ever did."

"Then why the fuck was he in my position. It's your family. You could've removed him at any time," I said angrily.

He chuckled. "It's not that easy."

"What the fuck is so difficult. The spot is mine anyway," I told him.

"Yes, it is. We chose Sanchez, because we knew he would die to remain head of the family. He would sacrifice his own to keep his position. You would die to save your family from this life. We needed someone who would hold the family together by any means necessary. I still need someone to head Maria's family."

"I'm not marrying her. The bitch knew about my drugs being stolen," I confessed to him.

"I know. Sanchez revealed that information to me before your arrival," he said. "She will marry Hector. He will take over her family business. I figure that will be punishment enough for her." I agreed with him. Hector will dog Maria out. He considered himself to be a player.

"What else did Sanchez tell you?" I asked.

"He says you think he killed Eduardo. He denies this. Without proof, I would have to let him remain in charge of the family. Now, I have to replace him."

Moreno ran this family on his own even though he was part of a cartel. He was the only one making decisions. His father left everything to him. I was surprised at how well organized he ran everything, because he was wild when he stepped up. "Why the fuck does the cartel have so much say in how you run your family?"

He smirked. "It's time for you to meet the rest of the family." I had no idea what he was talking about. I gave him a confused stare. "We will take a trip back to my home."

"My family?" I asked. I wasn't going anywhere until I knew they would be safe until I return.

"They will be safe for now. Come, the plane is waiting on us," he said standing up. I don't know what I was walking into. That wasn't my concern. I will die fighting for my family and Worth. "Can you please, tell your shooter to take the gun off me?"

I chuckled and looked at the red dot on Moreno's forehead. Guap was ready to take him out. I couldn't kill Moreno. Killing him was like killing everyone I loved. The cartel would kill everyone associated with me. I called Guap, and filled him in. I boarded Moreno's private plane not sure if I'd ever return.

Worth

"**W**orth, you have to tell him. You can't keep something like this from him. It's his child too," Paisley said as we sat in my car. I had just left my doctor's appointment confirming my pregnancy. I was only five weeks pregnant. I can't believe the fucked up situation I'm in. I'm in love and pregnant for a man that is marrying someone else. *So much for realizing my worth.* I thought as I sat in the car.

"I'm not going to tell him. I don't want him coming back to me, because I'm pregnant. He chose the life he's living over a life with me. I'll raise this child on my own," I said sternly.

"He's going to find out anyway. Eventually, Sheba's going to tell him. That's her brother's child. She's not going to keep this secret from him forever. Besides, he probably has someone watching your every move. He's going to find out. He's going to be furious you didn't tell him," she ranted.

"Well, let him find out on his own. I'm not going to tell him. If he didn't want a life with just me, he doesn't deserve a life with me and this child."

Natavia Presents

"That's not fair Worth, and you know it. You are being spiteful and vindictive."

I was and didn't care. "I'm done loving men who don't deserve my love. I love that man with every inch of my soul Paisley. I was willing to live his life with him. He walked away from me. He made his choice, and I'm making mine to move on with my life."

"Now look who's being bullheaded," she said shaking her head.

"Enough about me, what about you. Why didn't you tell Fila about being attacked?" I asked staring at her.

"I didn't think it was necessary. Besides I haven't seen or heard from him in a couple of days," she stated sadly.

"I told him," I confessed nervously.

Her big brown eyes grew wide. "Worth, why would you do that?"

"I'm sorry, He pried it out of me. He was asking questions about the bruises and bullet the hole in her wall. I tried to lie, but you know I'm no good at it."

"What did he say?" She asked.

"He was furious. He didn't say much about it though. I think he knows the guy that attacked you," I said.

"I have to go see him. I don't want him to do anything to get in any trouble." She looked so worried. "Take me home. I need to get my car."

"I'm sorry Paisley. I didn't mean to cause trouble," I said sincerely.

"It's not your fault. I made the mistake of going on a date with the guy," she said giving me a comforting smile.

"Paisley, stop running from him. Fucking another man will not make you forget how much you are in love with him."

"I know. I'm not going to run anymore. If it's a fight Estelle wants for his heart, I'm going to give her one," she stated boldly.

"That's my best friend," I said smiling as I drove.

"Speaking of best friends. I heard Tanika's pregnant. She doesn't know who the daddy is," Paisley said shaking her head. "I saw her the other day with a tall ass skinny nigga. He was cute though."

"Ugh, that's the asshole I saw her with. He treats her like shit," I said shaking my head. "I think I'm going to pick up baby Gladys for a couple of hours. Regardless of how I feel about her mother, she's still my Goddaughter and I love her little chubby self."

Natavia Presents

"Yeah , I'm sure that would make Lamar happy," Paisley said smiling. After dropping her off, I called Lamar to make sure it was okay to pick up Baby Gladys. I laughed to myself at how I always put the word baby in front of her name. I always told Tanika, it makes her name sound younger since she has such an old-fashioned name. Lamar said she was with his mother. I made plans to get her for the weekend.

I decided to head home. Love was coming over to spend the night with me. She wants to use my face for one of her tutorials. I stopped by the grocery store to get something to cook. I had a taste for some Shrimp Alfredo . After picking up everything I headed home. Sheba's car was backing out of my driveway as I was pulling in. She pulled forward when she spotted me. I parked my car beside hers. We both exited our vehicles.

"Hey sister in law," she said with a smile. I rolled my eyes at her and walked toward the front door. Her skin was a shade darker and glowing. I guess Jamaica was the perfect vacation for her. I didn't expect her back for a couple of days.

"I didn't expect you back for a couple of days," I said entering the house with her behind me.

"That was the plan, but shit seems to be crazy," she said. I quickly turned to face her. I was praying he was okay.

"Is he okay?" I asked.

"I'm sure he is. We haven't heard from him since we went on vacation. He said he wouldn't interrupt us while we were away." she said calmly. I breathed a sigh of relief. "We came back for Fila. It seems he got locked up." My heart dropped.

Paisley

I had searched everywhere for him. I've been to his house, carwash and all the other businesses that I know he owns. I couldn't find him anywhere. I rode by Estelle's house to see was his car there, but no one was home. I was starting to get worried. The only person I knew to ask was his father. He didn't know me at all for me to go knocking at his door. I only knew where he stayed, because Fila showed me one day when we were out joyriding. Unfortunately, his truck wasn't home when I went by there. I decided to head home, hoping he would come by. I know he was probably furious with me. Just as I pulled into my parking space my phone rang.

"Hey," I said answering Worth's call.

"Where are you?" She asked anxiously.

"I just got home. I can't find him anywhere Worth. I don't know where he can be. I hope he's okay."

She cleared her throat. "He's okay. Don't freak out. He was arrested last night. Dose is trying to get him out right now." My heart started beating rapidly.

"What happened? What was he arrested for?" I asked worriedly. Worth went on to tell me he was charged with aggravated assault. After hanging up the phone, I burst into tears feeling like this was all my fault. If I hadn't gone on that stupid ass date with Travis, he wouldn't be locked up.

She gave me the information of the precinct where he was being held. I started my car and headed in that direction. When I arrived, Fila was walking out with Dose and his father. I hurried and parked my car. I jumped out and rushed toward them. I wrapped my arms around his neck relieved to see that he was okay. I didn't feel his strong arms hugging me back. I unwrapped my arms from around his neck and looked at him. He stared down at me with a blank look on his face.

"I've been so worried about you. I've looked everywhere," I said staring at him.

"I'm good," he said nonchalantly.

"Yo, I'll get with you in the morning. We gotta look into this detective that tried to come for you. As for now, I know I don't have to tell you to stay the fuck away from Estelle's family," Dose said looking at him. Dose gave me a friendly smile. They gave each other a brotherly hug before Dose walked away to his car.

"You good?" His father asked him as we stood there.

"Gimme a few minutes," he told his father. His father nodded his head and walked away. I didn't like the look he was giving me.

"I-I can give you a ride home," I said nervously.

"Nah, I'm good. You were right Paisley. This shit between us ain't a good idea. My son comes before anything. This shit is making it hard for me to be there for him," he said shattering my heart.

"Please, don't do this. I was wrong. I shouldn't have gone on that date. I know I'm the reason you were locked up. I don't wanna end this. I didn't know he was Estelle's brother," I pleaded.

"I don't blame you. I shouldn't have started things with you until shit was settled with her. You have the right to date whoever the fuck you want. I won't stand in yo way," he stated with a coldness in his eyes. I didn't see the guy that told me he wasn't giving up on us. I saw a guy that looked at me as if I was just somebody he fucked.

"I don't want to date anyone else. I want you. I want us."

He ran his hand over his face and took a step back. "I ain't good for you right now, Paisley. I have too much shit going on."

"I know you are mad right now. I'm going to give you some time to cool off. I'm not walking away from you Fila. You told me you weren't walking away from me. I'm going to make you stick to that promise."

He chuckled as he stared at me. "That was before you tried to fuck another nigga." He walked off leaving me standing there speechless. I couldn't move my feet. I wasn't even able to turn around to watch him walk away from me. I was startled by someone tapping me on my shoulder. My heart jumped with joy thinking it was him coming back to me. I was wrong. It was his father.

"He's heated right now lil lady," he said smiling at me. I knew exactly how Fila would look when he got older. The only difference was his dad's gray hair in his hair and beard. "I'm Carl, his father. We haven't been formerly introduced."

I couldn't help but smile at him. He seemed like a kind man. "I'm Paisley." I reached out and shook his hand.

"I wouldn't be a gentleman if I left you standing out here in the dark alone. Get in your car. We'll follow you home," he said winking at me.

"He's never been mad at me before. Will he talk to me later?" I asked.

He grinned. "Yeah , he's just in a bad place right now."

"I didn't know that guy was her brother. I would've never gone on a date with him if I knew," I explained.

"It's not my place to discuss this with you, but I don't think the issue is him being Estelle's brother. The issue is you went on a date with another nigga," he said staring me in the eyes. I dropped my head in shame.

"Never hold your head down," he said lifting it up by my chin. "Besides there's more to the story than just Estelle's brother. I stared at him hoping he would give me answers. "Now, get in the car. I know that nigga starving." I giggled, because I'm sure he was. Fila could eat a damn horse, and still say he's hungry. Knowing him, I'm sure he didn't touch that jailhouse food.

Basilio

I thought I had seen some of the biggest mansions there was. Moreno's mansion made all the other's look like huts. We drove up a long, curvy, paved drive way. The perfectly landscaped lawn looked as if God created it himself. At the end of the driveway was two beautifully designed fence doors. The letter M was monogrammed on the metal fence doors. The entire mansion was surrounded by tall metal fences with white stone posts. The two gate doors opened, and the limo went through them. An enormous water fountain sat in the front of the mansion. The lawn was also landscaped with tall trees. The steps leading up to the tall double front doors were just as wide as they were long. The double doors were immediately opened when we made our way up the stairs. An elderly man wearing a butler's suit with white gloves on opened the door.

"Good evening Sir Moreno," he greeted Moreno with a head bow.

"Afternoon Miguel. We will be having a house guest for a few days. Treat him like family. This is Sir Vega," Moreno said introducing me. Miguel gave me a courteous head nod with a smile.

"Just call me Bull," I said to him .

"Yes sir," he replied.

"You can drop the sir," I told him. I hated to see housekeepers get treated like low class servants. I was a firm believer in treating the janitor the same way you would treat a CEO. The way I saw it we were no better than someone picking up trash. We spilled more garbage on the streets than they could pick up. He gave me a gracious smile.

"I will prepare your room," he said before walking away.

The castle style mansion was over the top. Being an architect, I couldn't help but be fascinated by the Mediterranean style mansion. The stairwell leading to the second floor was absolutely beautiful. Even though I loved the structure of the home, I wasn't impressed by the décor of the grand room that we entered. It was too flashy for such a classical architectural theme. The vibrant colors did no justice for the style of the home . There was a huge chandelier hanging from the ceiling that I couldn't help but admire.

"It's one of the few things that we didn't change in the house. We remodeled after our father died. I didn't like the mausoleum style the mansion had," a tall, slender beautiful woman said entering the room. I stared at her wondering who the fuck she was.

She gave me a gracious smile while sitting on a red contemporary style leather couch. She crossed her long legs and stared at me. Moreno sat on the other end of the couch. I could only assume this was his wife or girlfriend. I never knew if Moreno was married. He never mentioned a family outside of the drug family he leads. "Well, why didn't you just buy another home?"

She laughed. "We were forbidden to sell it in the will. Trust me, I wanted to. I feel like I'm living in a mausoleum."

"Why am I here?" I said wanting to get to the reason for bringing me here.

"We have business to discuss. It seems you have killed our second most profitable man. We have to decide on how to fix this. We can't just let you walk away that easy," she said with a stern face.

"And who the fuck are you?" I asked glancing at her and Moreno.

She laughed. "I'm the face behind the empire. My brother is only the image we present." I glanced at Moreno to see was she telling the truth. He couldn't look me in the eyes. "See, Moreno doesn't have the mindset to run this business like I do. That's why Father left me in charge. Even in this day and time, some men looked down on women running a drug empire. We decided to use Moreno as the face of our legacy."

"Let's not act like I can't run this shit. None of this would've happened if you had done as I said," Moreno said giving her a cold stare.

"We wouldn't have this empire if I listened to you," she said brushing him off. "Have a seat Mr. Vega." I stood there staring down at her as she remained seated. "Have it your way."

"You killed the leader of your family. He was your connect and brother. How do you think we should rectify this matter?" She asked.

I shrugged my shoulders. "I really don't give a fuck how you choose to fix it." She gave me a harsh stare.

"You will become the leader of the family. You will recruit new members that must be approved through us. If profits don't show you can run this family. I will kill you and your entire family."

I wasn't worried about whether or not I can run the family. I knew I could do that. My concern was wanting to be out of this life. I wanted to build my life with Worth.

"And if I say no I assume my family is dead." She nodded her head with a smirk.

"Maria is no longer in the family. The only members left are you, Hector and Chiraq. I've given Hector a month to improve his profits. He will not be given more territory until he can prove he can run the ones he has now. You have a month to bring in three more family members. I would advise you to think carefully on your choice. They are the ones that will determine your family's fate," she stated.

"What have you done to Maria?" Moreno asked staring at her.

"She betrayed the family. She will pay for her betrayal by working the fields," she said with a smile. *Damn!* Maria wouldn't last a day in the cocoa fields. She's never worked a day in her life. "Chiraq will not be given any more territory unless he agrees to negotiate his pricing. He is basically robbing us as it is. I will not continue to supply him at such a low price. My father was weak giving in to his demands." I chuckled.

Chiraq was a savage that she wasn't ready to fuck with. I didn't doubt her ability to lead. If she wasn't capable, the empire would've crumbled by now. I'm just not the man to lead their family. I thought I was ready to take the spot until I met Worth. There is nothing about this life that I would choose over her. My mind is already turning about how to bring Camila down. Her brother will be my greatest weapon.

"Oh, there's one other thing," she said standing up. "This young lady that you seemed to have fallen in love with, she is off limits. She is a distraction to your ability to run this family. If you disobey my orders, I will kill her."

1 week later

Fila

It's been a week, and no one has heard from Bull. We couldn't find Guap. One thing I learned while running with Bull and Dose was that Guap was never far away. Sheba was starting to worry. Dose tried not to show concern, but I could see it in his eyes. We had no information. Maria was also MIA. Dose didn't know what Bull's plan was since their plan got side tracked when Eduardo was killed. They thought they had Sanchez where he didn't have a choice, but to walk away when they found his kids. They were stuck waiting to see what Moreno had to say about the territories. After Eduardo was killed, Moreno put an end to the war between Bull and Sanchez.

"I knew I shouldn't have went on that damn vacation. I had a feeling he was up to some shit. He was persistent about us going away," Dose said as we sat in the VIP section at Bull's club.

"What the fuck you think he's doing?" I asked. We knew he wasn't dead. We were more concerned with him doing this shit on his own.

Natavia Presents

"I don't have a fucking clue. I know some shit has gone down since I've been gone. Too many mothafuckas MIA," Dose said shaking his head.

"Nigga, tell me you got some news for me," Dose said when Tree approached our table.

"That's what you pay me for ," he said taking a seat and smiling. We waited to hear what he had to say. "Guap followed Bull and Moreno to Colombia. Genius downloaded an app in Bull's phone to track him. I guess he had this plan in motion or something."

"Where the fuck is Guap now?" I asked anxiously.

"Held up in some cheap ass motel in Colombia. He says Bull is at Moreno's mansion. That's not the crazy shit though," he said smiling.

"Man, just fucking tell us," Dose said getting frustrated.

Tree leaned forward resting his elbows on the table. "Bull killed Sanchez in front of Moreno."

"What?" Dose and I said at the same time. Tree filled us in on everything Guap told him. Dose immediately called for a private flight to Colombia. He got the track phone number from Tree to call Guap. He called him to let him know he'll be arriving soon.

"What time we leaving?" I asked.

"Nah, you gotta stay here and handle shit with your son. And other matters," he said glancing over at Paisley who had entered the club with Worth. I hadn't spoken to her since the night I left the jailhouse. I've only seen Fiji once. The bitch got me having supervised visits with my son. I was relieved when he asked me when he can come home with me. I thought maybe he was mad at me for hitting his granny and beating his uncle. I wanted to sit down and try to explain everything to him, but I was forbidden to speak of the incident. It broke my heart that I couldn't take him home with me. I had to agree with Dose. I needed to stay here and handle this crazy shit with Estelle. Estelle called me to meet with her tomorrow for lunch. Pops thought it was a bad idea. I have to take a chance. I'm hoping to talk some sense into her about dropping the custody battle.

"What did you find out?" Sheba asked walking up to our booth.

"Chill Sheba, he's good. He's in Colombia handling business," Dose said only giving her half the story.

"Nigga, stop lying to me. I haven't heard from my brother in over a week. He would never go that long without talking to me or you. He doesn't even know Worth is carrying his child," she said sadly. I looked at her in disbelief. I had no idea Worth was pregnant.

"I'm getting ready to catch a flight in a few hours. Tree is going with me. Guap is already there watching Bull's back," Dose assured her.

"I'm going too," she stated.

"Nah, I need you here to keep an eye on Worth. You know if something happens to her that nigga will lose his damn mind," he told her. She smacked her lips, but she knew he was telling the truth.

"Bring my brother home," she demanded.

"Let your manager take over for the night. I'll fill you in on everything at the house," he said to her touching the side of her thigh. She melted in his hands and smiled.

After they departed , I debated on whether to walk over and speak to Worth and Paisley. She looked beautiful as always. I didn't care for the short ass dress she was wearing, but she looked damn good in it. Shit, she looked too damn good for these niggas to be looking at her. "What up Fila?" Tanika said approaching the table. She sat next to Tree.

"What the fuck you want?" He asked her.

"Something to drink," she said rolling her eyes at him.

He chuckled. "You got thousand-dollar weave in your hair, and can't buy a ten-dollar drink?"

"Yeah nigga, remember you paid for the hair too," she said calling him out.

I laughed. "Damn, you caking?" I asked looking at him.

"Ain't you buying Range Rovers?" He asked staring at me.

"For a lady not a…," I was interrupted by Tanika.

"So, is Paisley still fucking your brother in law. I heard you nearly killed him when you found out," she asked with a smile.

I chuckled. "She could fuck my daddy, and still wouldn't be a bigger hoe than you." Tree laughed.

"You just gone let him disrespect me like that?" She asked staring at him.

He shrugged his shoulders. "Shit, he ain't lying."

"Well, why you fucking with me then?" She asked him with an attitude.

"Because you a freaky ass hoe. Shit, you know that," he said winking at her with a smile.

"Fuck y'all," she said jumping up from the table and storming off. I stared at Tree. I could see what he was trying to hide.

Natavia Presents

"What?" He asked looking at me confused.

"Yo ass like her," I said smiling.

"Hell nah, she's a damn hoe. Bitch fucking about two other niggas in here," he said.

"Yeah , but you still like her," I reiterated.

"Man, fuck you. I'm not about to sit here and discuss my feelings with yo ass," he said getting up from the booth.

I laughed. "I bet you 'bout to go order that ten-dollar drink."

"Fuck you," he said walking off.

Paisley

"**A**re you going over and speak to him?" Worth asked as we sat at our booth. I've been watching Fila from the moment I arrived at the club. I haven't spoken to him in over a week. I tried calling him for two straight days, but he never answered my calls. I finally gave up. I decided if he wanted to talk to me, he would call. If he doesn't want to deal with me, then I will just move on. I can't apologize and make up for what I did if he's not willing to give me a chance.

"Nope, he wants to be petty and childish, so will I," I said before taking another shot. Worth couldn't drink because of her pregnancy. I decided to take advantage of having a designated driver and get wasted.

"You might as well go speak. You can't stop looking over there," Worth said jokingly. She was right. He looked so damn good just sitting there. He was dressed in a pair of light blue distressed jeans, a fitted tee shirt and cap. Of course, he wore his custom-made Fila sneakers.

"I'm not thinking about him," I lied.

"Whatever," she said laughing. My heart started to pound when he started walking in our direction. We both looked up at him when he approached our table.

"Hi Fila," Worth said smiling at him.

"Congratulations," he said winking at her with a smile.

"God, Sheba has a big mouth," she said angrily.

"That's her fam in there. You know she's excited," he said. He hadn't looked in my direction yet. I was eagerly waiting to see if he would at least acknowledge me.

"Well, at least my child will know somebody in its father's family," she said sadly.

"Stop tripping, you know that nigga gone be happy about his seed," he told her.

"Whatever, doesn't matter to me anymore," Worth tried convincing herself.

"You need anything, just let me know. And I hope you got that damn gun in a safe place," he said to her.

"Yup, when I bring it out I be ready to bust shit open," she said holding her hand like she was shooting a gun. He burst into laughter. He finally turned to give me some attention. I couldn't hide how nervous I was.

"Always beautiful," he said staring down at me.

I smiled at him. "Hi, how are you?"

"I'm good. Bout to get outta here. Got some shit to handle." I didn't want him to go…not without me.

"Can we talk?" I blurted out before I knew it. I hated I was acting like a needy female. It was obvious he wanted nothing to do with me, and I'm here begging for his attention. I was started to get angry with myself.

"Not tonight Pai…," he said before I interrupted him.

"Forget it," I said agitated with myself. All I wanted to do now was go home and forget I ever let myself love him.

"Worth, are you ready," I said before taking my last shot. I didn't realize how drunk I was until I stood up. I stumbled nearly falling.

"Woah," he said gently grabbing my arm to keep me from falling.

"I'm fine," I lied jerking away from him. "Let's go Worth," I said storming away from the table.

"Paisley slow down." I heard Worth saying trying to catch up with me. I was stopped by a pair of strong arms wrapping around my waist.

"Where you running off to slim thick?" the voice behind me said into my ear. His breath smelled horrible.

"Get your damn hands off me," I said trying to wiggle out his grip.

He laughed. "Shit, I'm trying to help yo drunk ass stand up." He wouldn't let me go as I struggled to get out his arms.

"Let her the fuck go!" Worth screamed trying to pull his arms off me.

"This yo bitch? You eating her pussy?" I heard him say to Worth. Before Worth could answer the guy's body went flying to the floor. I quickly turned around to see Fila standing over him.

"We gotta fucking problem here?" He asked staring down at the guy. He wiped blood from his mouth and stood up.

"Nah, we good," he said cutting his eyes at me.

"Take yo drunk ass home Paisley," he demanded staring at me. I know he didn't have the audacity to be mad at me.

"You don't tell me what to do. Nigga, I go and come as I please. Fuck you!" I yelled storming out the club.

Worth and I stood in front of the club waiting for the valet to bring her car. I could feel Fila's presence behind me. His strong sensual cologne couldn't be denied.

"Take her home with you Worth. She does stupid shit when she's not thinking clearly."

"Yeah , like fucking you! Biggest mistake I made!" I regretfully said turning to face him. All I wanted to do was fuck him until he remembers how good we are together.

"I guess rapist are more your preference," he said with a smirk.

"Y'all stop it. You both are acting like immature teenagers," Worth said scolding both of us.

Fila laughed. "I'll check on you both tomorrow. I have someone making sure you go straight home too." He looked at me. "Don't make me fuck you up Paisley. Remember who the fuck you belong to." As disrespectful as those words might have sounded, they were music to my ears.

Basilio

The past week has been hard being away from her and my family. Camila was determined to keep my mind on the family business. She confiscated my phone, and demanded I not contact anyone. To not risk their lives, I obeyed their rules. I knew I had eyes on me. That was the type of savage Dose trained in Guap. I knew he was somewhere here with me. I'm sure he's notified everyone to let them know what went down. I'm just patiently waiting on Dose and Fila's arrival. It will all pay off in the end. Camila is sending me back to the states in a couple of days to recruit three new family members. I already know who I'm bringing in. What she doesn't know is they will be the ones to help me bring her down. I have to convince them that I am on their team. I've been spending most of my time with Moreno. Camila instructed him to show me the operation on and off of the fields. What they didn't know was I already knew how the operation was ran. My goal was to get in their minds. I could tell Moreno didn't like that Camila ran everything. He didn't agree with the way she ran the empire. She looked down on Moreno. She didn't see him as fit to be the leader of the empire. I'm going to convince Moreno to eliminate her from power and let us take over. I have to be careful about the way I approach him with the idea. Even though he doesn't agree with his sister, loyalty is everything to him.

Today, we were out in the cocoa fields. I saw some shit that fucked with me mentally. As furious as I was with Maria for keeping information from me, I didn't like seeing her in the fields working. I loved her father like family and knew he wouldn't want to see his daughter being treated this way. The more I think about her actions toward me, the more I became less angry with her. She was in love with me . She wanted the plan to work, so I could marry her. I don't agree with her actions, but I can understand her logic. She wasn't a bad person. I guess she was just a young woman hoping to marry the man she thought she loved. I'll do my best to get her out this situation. I was interrupted from my thoughts by a knock on my bedroom door. I got off the bed and opened the door.

"Your family has arrived," Camila said with a straight face. She knew they were coming as well as I did. "Remember their lives depends on your actions." She turned and walked away. I could hear Moreno's voice as I made my way to the huge den. I was happy to see my brother, Dose. I kept a straight face as I entered the den. I greeted him with a brotherly hug.

"You straight?" He asked looking me over.

I laughed. "Yeah , I'm good. Moreno has been the perfect host." I was gradually trying to win Moreno's trust.

"Why the fuck we ain't heard from you?" Dose asked. "You know Sheba nagging the hell out of me about your whereabouts."

"My bad. House rules I had to keep my mind focused on business," I said with a smile.

Dose looked at me as if I was crazy. "What the fuck you all happy for? He got your ass here like a damn prisoner and you smiling like you on some shit or something. You done drunk some of that Jim Jones' Kool-aid in the jungle, nigga?"

"He's happy, because we are preparing to take over the drug industry," Camila said walking into the room.

"Who the fuck is this?" Dose asked looking Camila up and down.

"I'm the bitch that supplies you," she said taking a seat on the couch crossing her legs.

"What?" Dose asked looking back and forth at me and Moreno.

"This is my sister, Camila. Camila, I don't have to tell you who he is," Moreno said dryly.

"Man, tell me what the fuck is going on?" Dose said looking at me.

"You can tell your gunmen outside the gate they can put their weapons away. No one will be killed here. We welcome you to our home to discuss business," Camila said staring at Dose.

"Who you got?" I questioned on who was outside the gate.

"Tree, Guap and some soldiers. Nothing major," he said shrugging his shoulders.

"Fila?" I asked.

"Got some shit back home he needs to handle," he told me. I gave him a concerned look. "Nothing like that. He's good for now." I breathed a sigh of relief. I didn't want Fila taking out the game this soon. We had big plans for him.

"I'm sure you are here to take your brother home. He's not a prisoner here. We just needed his undivided attention while we discuss business," Camila said staring at me. She had been giving me a lustful look the last couple days. I had no interest in getting involved with her. She was a very beautiful woman but did nothing for me. Her slim frame had no curves. She had big brown eyes with long lashes. Her lips were pumped with too much collagen. She wore her long, silky black hair straight with a part in the middle.

"We need to know that you are with us on this take over. If not, Bull will have to choose our empire or his family," she said with a smirk.

"First of all, why the hell are you doing all the talking? Why the fuck is Moreno just sitting behind the desk like he doesn't have a say in this?" Dose asked staring at her.

"Because he doesn't," she said with a smile.

Dose looked at me for answers. "I'll explain later." I said to him. "Let's handle business. I got shit back home I need to handle."

"Remember our talk, Bull. No distractions," Camila saying referring to Worth. The bitch must be stupid as hell if she thinks she can keep me from the woman I'm doing this for.

2 days later

Paisley

"He's good!" I yelled, telling my dad as we watched my baby brother play in an AAU basketball tournament. He is a center with awesome power down low.

"Yeah , he's gotten better this season since he's put on some weight. We still trying to get about fifteen more pounds on him. He was like a damn noodle a year ago," Dad replied. He was slender but had muscles. I have been talking to my dad often. I still haven't told Mama that I've reconnected with him. I know she's going to flip out when I tell her. I jumped up and cheered my brother on as he made another three pointer. The buzzer rang ending the second quarter. Since it was half time, I decided to go to the concession stand to get a bottle of water.

"You want anything?" I asked Daddy standing next to him.

"Nah, I'm good Munchkin," he said smiling at me. I felt good bonding with him again. I could see how much he misses having me in his life. I didn't realize how much I missed having him in mine.

I was standing in line when I felt arms wrap around my legs almost causing me to fall. "Paisley!" I heard his happy little voice. I looked down to see Fiji smiling up at me. I couldn't help the big grin that spread across my face.

"Hi," I said lifting him up in my arms.

"Paisley, put me down. I'm a big boy. You can't be holding me like I'm a baby," he told me. I laughed and put him down.

"I miss you. Why you don't come see me no more?" He asked with a sad face.

I kneeled down to look in his eyes. "I miss you too. I've been very busy. I'm sorry."

He smiled. "That's okay. You can make it up to me by buying me some popcorn."

I laughed. "I can do that." I stood up and looked him right in the eyes. I stared at him as if he was the only person in the crowded concession area.

"You need to be more careful with him," I told him to break the awkwardness.

"What I tell you about running off from me?" He said looking down at Fiji.

"I'm sorry Daddy. I wanted to see Paisley. She say she miss me too," he said looking up at his handsome daddy with a big smile.

A Love Worth the Fight 3   Nona Day

Fila looked back at me. "Is he the only one you miss?"

I couldn't help but blush. "It depends on if anyone else misses me."

"Yeah , he misses you. He told me he does!" Fiji said pulling my hand to get my attention. I smiled not taking my eyes off Fila.

"What are you doing here?" He asked.

Before I could answer his question, I was nearly knocked off my feet. Estelle came and stood beside Fila. She stared at me with a smirk on her face. "I'm ready," she said wrapping her arm around Fila's arm.

"No, Paisley going to buy me some popcorn," Fiji said jumping up and down.

"We will buy you some popcorn. We need to go find a seat first, so we can watch the game," Estelle said glancing down at Fiji. It felt like my heart was caving in. I wanted to get as far away from them as I could.

"Maybe next time," I said looking down at Fiji. I looked up to see Fila staring at me. He was going to speak before Estelle interrupted him.

"Come on Fila, you said this was family night. Let's find a seat and enjoy the game with our son," Estelle said staring at me.

I wanted to whoop the bitch ass. She stood there smirking at me knowing her brother tried to rape me. It wouldn't surprise me if she convinced him to do it. The only reason my fist wasn't smashing into her face was because of Fiji. He had already watched his dad beat his uncle. He didn't need to see me beating his mom. "Enjoy the game, it's a good one," I said turning away from them.

"Paisley," I heard Fila's voice call my name.

I turned to face him. "No," was all I said glancing down at Fiji. I knew if another word came from Estelle's mouth I wouldn't be able to control my anger.

"Come on daddy. We gotta find a seat," Fiji said pulling Fila's arm. Fila reluctantly turned and walked away with Estelle on his arm. I can't believe he was here with her like nothing happened. This was what I was afraid of. I knew he would eventually go back to her.

I walked outside the gym to calm my nerves. About ten minutes later, I went back inside the gym. As if the night couldn't get any fucking worse, I looked to see Fila laughing and talking with Daddy. I desperately wanted to turn around and leave the gym, but I wanted to see Cedric finish his game. My feet felt like cement blocks as I made my way up the bleachers .

A Love Worth the Fight 3   Nona Day

"I thought you had left," Daddy said as I sat beside him. Fila, Fiji and Estelle were sitting above us. The second half had already started.

"It's good to see the weight ain't slowing him down," Fila said referring to one of the players.

"Yeah , that was our biggest concern. It's damn sho helping him control the board," Daddy said making me realize Fila was talking about Cedric. I wanted to ask Daddy how he knows Fila, but I remained quiet. I didn't want to get into any beef with Estelle.

"Yeah , that was a foul!" I jumped up and yelled at the referee when the center from the other team bumped Cedric too hard.

"I don't like these seats. We need to find somewhere else to sit," I heard Estelle say.

"Nah, we good right here. These the best seats in the house," Fila said.

"Fair warning Munchkin, he gets mad with his mother when she yells out," Daddy said laughing.

"I don't care. He might as well get used to it," I stated smiling.

"You know Ced?" Fila asked me. I turned to face him. Daddy answered proudly before I could.

"Yeah , this my daughter. He's her baby brother."

"Get the fuck outta here," Fila said surprisingly. I turned back around to watch the game. I could feel Estelle burning holes through me with her eyes.

"You know Munchkin?" Daddy asked Fila.

"Munchkin?" Fila asked with a laugh . I looked over my shoulder and rolled my eyes at him.

"Yeah , that's my nickname for her," Daddy told him. They both laughed.

"How exactly do you two know each other?" I asked glancing at them.

"Fila is the team's biggest sponsor. He lets them work out at his gym for free. He built a basketball court inside the gym just for the team," Daddy bragged on Fila. I didn't even know he owned a gym. I glanced at Fila and he winked his eye with a smile. My phone vibrated in my hand. I looked at the screen.

I love your kinky puff ball as much as I love you- Fila

I laughed at his remark about the big puff ball on top of my head. I stopped him from calling my hair nappy. Now, he calls it kinky. Daddy looked at me with a smile. "What?" I asked looking back at him.

He chuckled. "Nothing." We both started back watching the game.

Worth

"Worth, wake up. Someone is breaking in," Love whispered as she shook me out of my sleep. My heart jumped as I sat up in the bed.

"Sssshhh," I said putting my finger to my lips. I immediately heard the bumping downstairs. I jumped out of the bed and hurried over to the safe in the wall. I opened it and retrieved my gun.

"What are you doing with a gun?" Love asked staring at me as if I was a crazy woman.

"Protecting myself" I checked the gun like Sheba taught me. "Stay in here," I said walking toward the door.

"No, I'm not letting you go down there by yourself," she stated. "I need a gun too."

"No, you do not." I walked over to the bed and grabbed the bat from under it. "Here take this." She took it from me and followed me out the bedroom door. The house was pitch black. This is the one thing I hate about living in an enormous house. Someone could be living here with me and I would never know it unless I saw them with my own eyes. We tiptoed down the hall and stairs. I heard noises coming from the den.

"Stay behind me," I instructed softly to Love.

"Ok."

Once we made it to the double doors that led inside the den, I pushed them open. I saw the silhouette of the robber as he turned to face us. I immediately started shooting my gun. I heard him cry out in pain. I knew I had hit him when his body dropped to the floor. Love ran from behind me and toward the robber. She started beating him with the bat. I rushed over and flipped the light switch. *Shit!*

"Oh my God! It's Bull!" Love said staring down at him. He lay on the floor holding his arm.

I ran over to him. "I'm so sorry, I thought you were a burglar." I kneeled down beside him to see where I shot him.

He immediately jumped up. "Where the fuck did you get a gun? You could've fucking killed me Bella." He snatched the gun from my hands and stared at me in disbelief.

"I thought someone was breaking in," I tried explaining as I stared at the blood seeping through his shirt. "We have to get you to a doctor. You are bleeding."

He looked at his arm. "It's just a flesh wound. Have you lost your damn mind?"

Now, I was furious. He has no right coming in here getting angry at me for protecting myself. "No, I'm perfectly damn sane. I have to have some protection in this big ass house. Remember, I was left here by my damn self, Basilio."

"There's men guarding this house twenty-four seven. You are never damn alone," he said angrily.

"I'll go get a first aid kit," Love said rushing out the room.

"The fucking bat hurt more than the gun shot," he said grabbing his side.

"I don't know what you mad for. You should be happy I'm able to defend myself," I stated with an attitude.

"I need a damn drink," he said marching over to the bar. He poured a shot of Tequila and downed it. He downed two more shots before he turned to face me.

"Who gave you a gun?" He asked staring at me.

"I bought it myself. I've been going to the gun range," I confessed. I wasn't going to rat Sheba out.

"Did you really think I would leave you here unprotected, Bella?" He asked hurtfully.

I didn't have a reply. It hit me all of a sudden that he was here. I didn't think I would ever see him again. If I did see him, I never imagined it would be this soon.

Natavia Presents

"Why are you here?" I asked staring at him. Before he could answer Love came back into the den.

"I have the first aid kit," she said handing it to me.

"Take off your shirt," I told him.

"Since everything is cool down here, I'm going to bed," Love said dismissing herself. She turn back around. "Oh, sorry about beating you with the bat, Bull." He nodded his head accepting her apology.

I helped him pull his shirt over his head. My flood gates opened as I stared at his masculine, sculpted body. I could feel my panties becoming damp. I was stuck. I stood there staring at him. There was nothing about this man that I didn't love. He cleared his throat to get my attention. I snapped back to reality. I sat beside him on the couch opening the first aid kit. He placed his hand on side of my face. I looked up at him. We sat there staring into each other's eyes without speaking a word. With his hand on my face, his thumb stroked my cheek.

"Bella," he said seductively. I wanted to feel his hands all over my body. The thoughts of his tongue caressing my womanhood was causing a thud between my legs. I quickly reminded myself that he belonged to another woman.

"I have to get a wet washcloth to clean the blood," I said jumping up from the couch. I exited the den and hurried to the bathroom. I needed to calm the urges stirring between my thighs.

Basilio

The moment I returned to New Orleans all I wanted to do was see her. I could never get enough of looking in her eyes. Worth was different from any woman I've ever been with. She was simple and innocent with a fire inside her that set a flame to my heart. I remember my old man telling me that when I find the kind of love he had with my mother, I wouldn't be able to deny it. I tried convincing myself my money and father's legacy was more important than love. I can't believe she got a gun and knows how to shoot it. I wasn't stupid. I know Sheba has something to do with her owning a gun. I made my way to the bathroom. She was standing there wiping tears from her face. I couldn't stand that I was the reason for those tears. I stood behind her wrapping my arms around her waist.

"Don't cry Bella," I whispered in her ear.

"I can't do this with you. You have to leave," she said looking at me through the bathroom mirror.

"I can't leave. This is where I belong. None of it is worth it, without you," I told her.

She turned to face me. "You are marrying another woman. I can't be the other woman. My love for you pumps through every vein in my body, but I love myself just as much."

"I'm not marrying Maria. I'm going to make it possible for us to have a life together," I said.

Her eyes widened as she stared at me. I moved closer to her barely leaving space between us. I realized she was wearing one of my tee shirts that swallowed her thick body. My hands slowly started lifting her shirt up her thighs. She stopped me by slapping the hell out of me across the face. She slapped me so hard I could taste my blood on the inside of my mouth . She pushed me in the chest. I was caught so off guard by her reaction, I stumbled backwards. "You will not keep walking in and out of my life! You left, so stay gone. I don't want you here anymore!"

I knew her words were coming from a place of hurt, but they still stung me. I moved toward her, and she started throwing blows at me. I gently grabbed her wrist to restrain her from hitting me. "I'm gone make this work, Bella. You have to give me a chance."

"You promise?" She asked with tear filled eyes.

"I promise." I wrapped my arms around her holding her tight. I could feel her body relaxing in my arms. I started placing soft wet kisses on her neck. She didn't stop me from touching her this time. I gripped the bottom of the tee shirt and pulled it up to her waist. She was wearing a pair of baby blue colored boy shorts. She stepped back and lifted her shirt over her head. Her full succulent breast sat up perfectly. Her juic fat mound caused my mouth to water. I walked to her and slid my tongue inside her sweet mouth. I groaned from the pleasure of being close to her again. She wasted no time sucking my tongue inside her mouth. Our tongues wrestled inside each other's mouths as my hands massaged and caressed her breast. Without breaking our kiss, I slowly started sliding her boy shorts down. I broke our kiss and started licking and sucking on her neck making my way to her hard nipples. Sounds of whimpering escaped her mouth as I softly bit them as I slid two fingers between her soaked lower lips. My fingers violated her swollen clit until she was coming in ecstasy. I grabbed her by the waist and sat her on the bathroom counter. My dick grew more as I stared down at her cream covered pussy lips. I quickly pulled her panties completely off and pushed her legs up in the air. She leaned back, resting against the bathroom mirror. I dove inside her creamy wet pussy like a scuba diver. Her body shivered when my tongue licked and slurped the sweet, wet creamy mixture from her pussy. I pushed her knees up to the side of her head giving me full access to her sweetness. I became a human tornado twirling my tongue between her meaty folds. I lapped my tongue up and down her pussy licking up all the sweet juices she was releasing. Slurping and sucking sounds echoed in the bathroom as I continued to gulp down every drop from her. My mouth covered her pussy as I sucked on her clit. I slid two fingers inside her drenched tunnel stroking her soft spot. Her body quaked as she exploded screaming out in pleasure. Determined not to waste a drop, I stroked my tongue between her voluptuous ass cheeks slurping up the sweet cream that escaped my mouth. Her sweat covered body jerked as I licked her clean.

I unfastened my jeans to release my brick hard dick. It sprung out of my boxers like a caged animal. A loud grunt escaped my mouth when she wrapped her soft hand around my shaft. She started licking her lips wanting to slide me inside her mouth. As much as I wanted to feel her soft lips around my dick, I wanted to feel the inside of her tight wet tunnel. I placed the crown of my dick at her tunnel and slowly slid inside her tightness. She wrapped her arms around me burying her face into my neck. She moaned as I groaned from the pure jubilation of being inside each other. She felt so damn hot and wet. I started sliding my throbbing dick in and out of her. Her warm liquids spilled out of her onto the counter every time I slid out of her.

"Siempre serás mia *You'll always be mine*, Bella" I said as she moaned into my neck while releasing her sweet essence on me. Looking down to see my rock-hard dick coated with her cream caused my dick to spread wider as I slid inside her. She unwrapped her arms from around me resting them behind her on the counter. She leaned back throwing her head back as she started gyrating her hips. I gripped her by the waist as she lifted her ass off the counter. I released a loud grunt that echoed throughout the bathroom when she clinched her walls around my rod as she twirled her hips. I started driving inside her magical walls faster and deeper. The deeper I went, the quicker she came. Back to back orgasms was causing tears to run down her cheeks.

Her body quivered. "Shiiiiittt! I'm coming again!" she screamed as her body stiffened and trembled. I pulled her into my arms holding her limp sweaty body. I couldn't hold my nut any longer. I slammed into her cream filled valley repeatedly until I felt the tingle in my spine. My toes cramped up and my stomach tightened .

"Gggggrrrrrrr Fuuuccccckkkk!" I roared releasing inside her. We held on to each other's sweat covered bodies until we were able to speak and move.

"I love you," she whispered softly in my ear. Those three little words from her caused my soft dick to jump and start hardening again.

Fila

"**D**on't think you slick nigga, I know you were texting her at the game," Estelle said as we drove to her mother's house. The damn house where I was paying the bills. I know damn well she doesn't think I'm going to keep paying the bills when they are the reason I was locked up.

"Last time I checked I pay my damn phone bill," I said glancing at her. I peeped in the rear view mirror to see was Fiji still awake. I wasn't going to argue with her in front of my son. That's the last thing he needs to see now.

"That bitch ain't shit. She was fucking my brother and you at the same time," she said trying to convince me Paisley was fucking Travis. I knew she only wanted to get under my skin.

"Estelle, chill out with all that. I don't want him seeing us argue. He's been through enough already. You asked to go to the game with us and I took you. Don't get this shit twisted between us." I know damn well she wasn't thinking I was considering giving us another try. The only reason she was with us was because she asked me in front of Fiji. He was so happy about us spending time together as a family I couldn't say no.

She folded her arms and pouted as she looked straight ahead. The remainder of the ride was quiet until we pulled up in front of her mother's house. "Pookie is here!" Fiji yelled excited to see his little cousin. Travis had a son a year younger than Fiji. The little boy's mother dropped him off one day and hauled ass. Now, he drops the little boy off when and wherever he can.

"Woah!" I said stopping him as he tried to hurry out the truck.

"Papa is coming to scoop you up next Friday to stay the weekend with him," I told him. I hated that I couldn't take my son home with me. The only reason I was trying to be nice to Estelle was to convince her to drop the stupid ass custody battle.

"Why can't I come stay with you?" He asked with a sad face. I glanced at Estelle and she rolled her eyes and looked out the passenger window.

I took a deep breath. "I wish you could Fiji, but you know I got into some trouble with the police. They wanna make sure it's safe for you to be at my house."

A big smile appeared on his face. "I'll tell them it's safe, then I can come stay." It was hard explaining adult bullshit to a child. I wish it was as simple as him telling them he wants to be with me.

"Gimme a hug and go see yo lil cousin," I said smiling at him. He reached around the seat giving me a big hug before jumping out the car. Estelle was still sitting there. "You can go too."

"I need to talk to you," she said with an attitude. I sat there waiting for her to speak. I had somewhere to be and she was wasting my time. "Ma said the rent hasn't been paid."

I looked at her to see if she was serious. She was. I burst into a fit of laughter. She sat there mean mugging me until I stopped laughing. I stared her in the eyes. "You can't be serious right now."

"She has an eviction notice," she stated.

"I don't give a damn. Your family is the reason I have supervised visits with my son and was arrested. I'm not paying a damn thang. Tell her to get one of those lil fuck boys to pay her bills," I told her.

"You haven't deposited any money into my accounts," she said.

I smiled. "I know. The only money you'll be getting from me is child support which is being handled by the courts. This is what you wanted so live with it."

"I can't live off that money. What do you expect me to do?" She asked in disbelief.

I shrugged my shoulders. "Drop the bullshit ass custody battle. Once that is done, we can negotiate."

"You are doing all this, so you can fuck that black nappy headed bitch," she stated angrily.

"Nah, I'm doing this because your family ain't shit. You paid a girl twenty-five thousand dollars of my money to keep quiet about your brother raping her. Out of love for you, I was paying a grown ass, ungrateful woman's bills who don't do shit for herself. And then there is you, we both know the fucked up shit you did. As far as Paisley goes, she's the damn bonus in this fucked up situation." She reached over to slap me, but I grabbed her by her wrist. Travis had raped a young girl down the street that had a crush on him. I will admit the girl was a little wild. When I talked to her, I knew she was telling the truth. I found out Estelle gave him the money when I deposited money into her account. When I got the balance, I noticed the big drop in her balance for the month. The only reason I found out was Shawna told me. I wanted to beat that nigga into the ground. From that point on, I made sure to check her accounts to make sure she wasn't giving her family money. I only paid the rent and utility bills.

She laughed and snatched her wrist from me. "Majesty was right. You are a punk nigga." She opened the car door and jumped out the car. She slammed the door so hard the window cracked. The only thing I did was laugh. She wanted to infuriate me enough to get arrested again. I wasn't going to give her the satisfaction. Honestly, I didn't give a damn what she thought of me. Majesty would've said anything to get between her legs, and she fell for it. I pulled out the driveway as she stormed inside the house.

I kept calling Paisley's phone as I drove to her house only to be sent to voicemail repeatedly. I know it pissed her off seeing Estelle with me tonight at the game. I could see the hurt in her eyes. I was shocked to find out Cedric was her brother. I had started sponsoring the AAU basketball team three years ago. When Cedric joined the team a couple years ago, I immediately took a liking to his game. I knew with the right kind of help he could improve his game enough to go to a division one college. I met her dad at one of his games. We would sit and discuss Cedric's game as we watched him play. This was the first game I've ever seen Paisley attend. It made me wonder why she's never attended any of her brother's games before today. I was getting ready to call her phone again when my phone rang.

"Yeah," I said answering the call.

"He's awake," said the nurse at the hospital where Travis was being kept. It was a relief to know he was awake. The last thing I needed on me was a murder charge.

"Let me know when the family leaves," I instructed her.

She laughed. "Shit, ain't no family been up here to see this nigga." It didn't surprise me. That was the type of family they were. They were only there for each other when it was something in it for them. "There is a cop that wanted to know when he wakes up. I'm sure he's on his way over here."

"Let me know when he leaves. I don't care how late it is. Call me," I instructed her.

"I gotcha," she said ending the call. I'm sure the cop she was referring to is Detective Bailey. I've gotten word he's been asking questions about me.

Paisley

"I can't believe you finally came to one of my games," Cedric said as I drove him home. After the game, we went out to eat dinner together. He filled me in on how his high school years are going. I talked about my dreams to open my own hair salon and natural hair care product line. I found out he was a LeBron fan, while I was a Curry fan. He hopes to go to college at Michigan State on a full basketball scholarship. From what I saw today that should be no problem. He was only going to the eleventh grade and was a beast on the court.

"I must say all that hard work in the backyard paid off. I taught you well," I said smiling as I glanced at him.

He laughed. "It did. You know, I used to love to go to your basketball games and watch you play. You are the reason I worked so hard. I would tell myself I wanted to be just as good as my big sister one day."

I smiled at him. "Thank you." I've never had anyone to look up to me. It meant a lot to hear him say those words.

"Why did you stop playing? You could be playing pro now," he asked.

I shrugged my shoulders. "I don't know. I just lost interest in playing."

"Was it because of me?" He asked. I gave a puzzled look. I had no idea why he would think he was the reason I stopped playing.

"No, why would you think that?" I asked as I pulled into their drive way.

"When I started playing on a recreational team you stopped coming around. I used to want you to go to practice with me and come see my games. You never did. I thought maybe you were mad because Dad was spending time with me now."

"Oh my God, no Ced. I never felt that way. I'm sorry for making you feel that way. I was going through things that I kept to myself. I had a hard time dealing with not having my dad full time. I blamed him for leaving us. I stopped coming around because I was angry with him. It had nothing to do with you. I love you. I just couldn't handle watching him be a full time Dad to you when I only got him part time. I held a lot of my feelings inside, instead of talking to him about them."

"And now?" He asked.

I smiled. "I have my great Dad and an awesome brother in my life again." A big smile spread across his face. "And yo ma ain't too bad as a stepmom." He laughed.

"I heard them talking about buying you a car. He said you won't let him," he told me.

"I don't need him to do that. I have the money and credit to buy a car. I'm just trying to decide what I want. I'm truly thankful they offered but it's not necessary," I said. The reason I hadn't purchased a car yet is because I had become spoiled. After driving my dream truck that Estelle destroyed, I hadn't found a car that measured up to it. I knew my pockets weren't deep enough to buy myself one. Not yet anyway. Achieving my goals will make that happen in the future.

"At least let them make the down payment. It'll really make him happy. I can see how happy he is to have you back in his life. I don't know who's the happiest me or him. I always liked having a big sister," he said smiling. My brother is a handsome, young gentleman. I must say they did a great job raising him. I reached over and gave him a hug and kiss on the cheek.

"I guess it's cool having a little brother," I said jokingly. His phone was going off nonstop.

Natavia Presents

"I guess you have all the girls blowing your phone up since you are the big basketball star," I said after breaking our embrace.

"Yeah , they looking for a meal ticket," he said.

I laughed. "That sounds like something your mom would say. She's right. You have to be careful. These girls know you are headed to the Pros . Make sure you use your own condoms. Bitches be poking holes in condoms to trap niggas."

"Ma done ran the law down to me," he said smiling. I nodded my head.

"Anyone special?" I asked. He shrugged his shoulders. "Who?" I asked.

"She's a year older. She flirts with me, but doesn't take me seriously. She says I'm too young and have too many girlfriends."

I laughed. "Let me see a pic of her." I scrolled through his phone until he found her pic. He handed me the phone and I burst into laughter. I couldn't stop laughing. This city was beginning to be too damn small.

"What?" He asked staring at me. "You don't think she's pretty?"

I stopped laughing. "She's absolutely beautiful. I'm laughing because she's my best friend's sister." He looked at me in shock. "If she gives you a chance, you better treat her right. She's a nice girl."

"You gone put a good word in for me?" He asked smiling.

"I'll see what I can do," I said smiling and winking at him. "That's her you texting?"

He smiled. "Yeah ."

"Good night knucklehead," I said. He gave me another hug before exiting the car. It felt good having my brother and father back in my life.

The only problem I had now was forgetting the man I saw earlier today. I tried not thinking about him as I drove home, but I couldn't stop thinking about him. I don't know why I was shocked to see his car parked in my parking space when I pulled up to my apartment building. He exited his vehicle the same time as I stepped out mine. "No Fila! Take yo ass home to your family. I'm not doing this shit with you!" I said storming toward him. All he did was look down at me and smile. He took my keys out my hand and threw me over his shoulder. I kicked and screamed for him to put me down. He ignored me as he unlocked my apartment door. He put me down once we were inside.

We stared at each other without speaking until he finally broke the silence. "Sit down Paisley." I know that look in his eyes. He wasn't leaving. I walked over and flopped down on the sofa. He sat down beside me and pulled me on his lap. I struggled to get up, but he held me down. "Be yo stubborn ass still." I exhaled in frustration.

"Why are you here?" I asked.

"I'm sorry about the night at the jailhouse. I was in a fucked up place and said some fucked up shit to you," he said.

It always amazed me how soft he was with me. Fila was known in the streets as a savage. Niggas knew not to fuck with him. I never saw that side of him. "I never fucked him. I just wanted to stop thinking about you. It seemed like I was pulling you in a direction away from your child. I didn't want that on my conscience . I didn't want to be the reason she kept him from you. I did all that and I'm still the reason she's keeping you from him."

"No one is going to keep me from my son Paisley. That's not your fight to worry about. There's only one thing I need to know from you," he said staring at me.

"What?" I asked.

"I need to know that you got me. I don't need to worry about whether you gone ride this shit out with me or run because you scared of getting hurt. I'm not gone hurt you Paisley," he said with a stern face.

Natavia Presents

"How can I trust that when I see you out having family time with her. She was holding on to you like y'all was a couple," I told him.

"That was the only way I could convince her to let me take him to the game. All my fucking visits with him are supervised unless she's with us," he confessed.

"Why?" She asked. I filled her in on everything that happened as she straddled my lap. After I was done, she confessed and told me about Estelle asking her to leave me alone.

"I got a trifling ass baby mama and a dirty ass detective coming for me Paisley. I love you but if you want out I'll understand. If you stay in this with me I need to know you got me the same way I got you." For the first time since I've become involved with him, all the doubt I've ever felt was gone. I wanted to give myself a chance to be loved by him.

I leaned forward and sucked his bottom lip into my mouth. He conquered mine with his. I broke our kiss when I pulled his shirt over his head. I could feel the wetness between my thighs spilling into my panties. We wrestled with each other's clothing until we were both naked. The next thing I knew, I was sliding down on his thick rod. He filled up every inch of me. Goosebumps popped up on my flesh from the exhilaration of feeling him inside me. He cupped my breast massaging them as he licked and sucked on my nipples. I buried his head further into my breasts as I rocked back and forth on his one-eyed monster. Every nerve in my body was heightened by the feeling of his thick dick sliding in and out of me. I could feel myself getting ready to explode as I sped up my pace rocking back and forth.

"Shit! You riding the fuck out my dick!" He moaned as he gripped the sides of my waist. One thrust of his hips and I was screaming his name as I came. "Fuck!" He roared before he started bouncing me up and down his steel hard dick. Sloppy gushing sounds sounded through the room as I felt my juices splattering on us. He was hitting every sensitive spot inside me as he slammed me up and down.

"Oh shiiitt! I'm 'bout to come Fila!" I screamed as my mouth watered.

"Who pussy is this Paisley?" He demanded as he continued to bring me pure bliss. "Shit, this pussy good and tight!"

"It's your pussy Fila. It's all yours!" I screamed before my eyes rolled to the back of my head. My mouth fell open, but no sound came out. He lifted me up and laid me on the sofa spreading my legs apart. My soul left my body when his tongue started licking and slurping between my pussy lips. I screamed and cussed as my body went through unimaginable ecstasy.

"Damn, I can't get enough of your taste," he mumbled as he continued to suck and slurp. Tears poured down the side of my face, unable to control myself from coming repeatedly. He didn't want to stop, and I didn't want him to stop. I just didn't know how much more my body could take of the agonizing pleasure he was giving me. He quickly flipped me over, positioning me on all fours . He spread my ass cheeks and his tongue became a magic wand around my anus as he slipped two fingers inside my dripping wet pussy. I was so hot and turned on by what he was doing to me I was begging for him to put it in. He placed the head to my drenched hole.

I looked over my shoulder at him. "Get a condom, for the other one."

His eyes widened as he stared at me in shock . "You serious?" I nodded my head yes.

"Shit!" He barked as he rambled through his wallet until he pulled out a condom. I thought he would get a condom from my nightstand . I was too hot to interrupt this moment to discuss why he had a condom when we don't use protection. I watched him slide it on his thick, long rod. He started lapping his tongue from the top of my crack to my wet pussy until I was begging him again. I never had anal sex before and don't know what caused me to want to try it now, but I wanted it. He placed the head of his dick at my entrance and my body immediately tensed up.

"Relax for me baby," he said sliding a finger inside my hole while he massaged my clit with his other hand. Eventually one finger became two and I was gyrating my hips from the feeling of his fingers in my ass. After a few minutes, he pulled them out. He slowly and gently started sliding his head inside me. I started regretting my choice to experience this with him. I never imagined it would hurt this much. I wanted to tell him to stop but I asked for this. Slowly and gently he slid more and more inside me. The feeling of him caressing my clit was starting to relax me more. I didn't realize I was gyrating my hips until I heard a loud grunt come from him. I looked over my shoulder to see his eyes closed and face contorted. That gave me the motivation to take what he was giving me. I started rocking my hips causing him to slide in and out of me. The more I rocked back and forth the better he felt inside me. My low moans were mixed with his groans as pleasure took over my body. My body relaxed as I adjusted to his size. I became more aggressive pumping my ass as I felt myself getting ready to explode. This feeling was different. It felt like electric shock waves were shooting through my body as the orgasm built up.

"Got damn! Ooooohhhh Ssssshhhit!" He bellowed slapping my ass. He squeezed my ass cheeks and lost control inside me. I wasn't complaining. I enjoyed every thrust he gave me.

"Aaaaaahhhh!" I screamed as we both came. All I could do was collapse on the sofa.

Worth

I lay in bed with my eyes still closed. I was afraid to open them. I didn't want to wake up to the reality that last night was only a dream. The scent of his cologne lingered in the air. I slowly opened my eyes and looked to my side to see was he laying next to me. My heart dropped when I didn't see him. I sat up in the bed resting my back against the headboard. I started praying to God to take these feelings away from me. I didn't want to love him as much as I did. My stomach growled reminding me I was eating for two. I smiled as I placed my hand on my belly looking down at the little life growing inside me. I couldn't understand how my heart could be broken and whole at the same time. I lost my soulmate but gained a life inside me at the same time. I was taken from my thoughts when the bathroom door opened. A big smile appeared on my face when he walked out with a towel wrapped around his waist. He walked over, leaned down and kissed me on the lips.

"Afternoon," he said smiling at me.

"What time is it?" I asked. I couldn't help but stare at his wet, sculpted body. It seemed like it was more defined than the last time I was with him.

"Almost two o'clock," he said sitting on side of the bed. "You want to tell me why you were looking so sad?"

I dropped my head. I wanted to tell him about the baby, but I wanted to be sure he was back to stay for just me. "I thought last night was just a dream when I didn't see you in the bed with me."

He lifted my chin for me to look him in the eyes. "I'm here Bella. I'm where I want to be."

"For how long this time Basilio?"

He took a deep breath. "Everything I'm doing is for us. I will be back and forth for a little while."

I immediately became angry. I raised my legs and kicked him off the bed. He flopped down on the floor. "You said you wasn't marrying her."

"You better be glad I love you Bella." He got up off the floor and stared down at me. "I'm not marrying Maria. If you can control your hot temper, I will tell you what's going on." I sat there huffing with my arms folded. He sat on the edge of the bed and stared at me. "Your emeralds are sparkling." He winked his eye and I rolled both of mine . My stomach growled, and he started laughing, only infuriating me even more.

"Come, let me feed you first," he said getting up off the bed.

A Love Worth the Fight 3   Nona Day

"Oh, you cooking me breakfast?" I asked sarcastically. He nodded his head yes. I wanted to see this. I wasn't going to lift a finger to help him either. After taking a shower, I got dressed and went downstairs. The delicious aroma coming from the kitchen caused my stomach to growl even more. I was shocked when I walked into the kitchen to see Sheba and my mom cooking. I looked at Basilio and he gave me a devilish grin.

"Hey baby," Mommy said turning to face me. I walked over and gave her a big hug.

"What are you doing here?" I asked.

"I can't come see my baby?" She asked breaking our embrace. There was something different about my mother. She looked relaxed and happy.

"Of course, you can. It's just that every time I ask, you always decline my offer," I reminded her.

"I'm sorry. I'll start coming more often. Bull was nice enough to let me in. He said he heard your stomach growling in your sleep, so I offered to cook lunch. Sheba just happened to stop by and offered to help me. She wants to learn how to cook New Orleans style food," Mommy said with a smile. I rolled my eyes at Basilio again.

He walked over to me. "That's exactly how your eyes roll into the back of your head when you coming on my dick," he whispered in my ear. My mouth dropped open in disbelief that he said that. "I'm going to leave you to enjoy your mother and sister in law. I promise we will talk later."

"Where are you going?" I asked.

"Nowhere Bella. I'm expecting some guests tomorrow. Until then, I'm all yours," he said winking his eye before walking away. I watched him as he walked toward the study. I wanted to be happy about him being here, but something kept telling me not to get too excited.

"What are you cooking?" I asked giving Mommy and Sheba my attention.

"I'm learning to make Gumbo," Sheba said excitedly. I smiled as I sat at the kitchen table.

"Here eat a couple of these until we're done," Sheba said placing a plate of oyster Rockefeller on the table. They looked delicious.

"You made these?" I asked her. She nodded her head yes. I was skeptical about trying one. I didn't want to hurt her feelings if they weren't good. I slipped one into my mouth. I was shocked.

"Sheba, this is delicious," I said smiling at her.

"I'm a quick learner like you," she said winking at me. I knew she was referring to me learning to shoot. I laughed.

"It'll be done in about twenty minutes," Mommy said sitting at the table with me. I was so happy to see her in my house.

"Where's Love?" I asked looking around.

"She had to go do some makeup," Mommy said. Love was becoming very popular with her face beating skills. "Oh yeah , and I left your father." I stared at her unable to reply. "When is the baby due?" I immediately stared at Sheba furious she would tell my mother something so personal.

"Don't be looking at me like that. I didn't say anything," Sheba said smiling at me.

"Chile, I'm your mother. I know your body better than you do. Besides, I've had two kids myself. I know when a woman is pregnant. Your skin is glowing and your breasts and hips are spreading," she said looking at me.

"I'm sorry Mommy. I know you wanted us to wait until we are married," I said shamefully.

"Yes, I did but there's no need to be sorry. Babies are a blessing. Are you happy about it?" She asked. I nodded my head yes. "Well that's all that matters. Now, you need to tell that man you carrying his child. It's not fair to keep it from him."

"How do you know I haven't told him?" I asked.

She smiled. "Because, he's not walking around here with his chest stuck out. Men love to gloat about getting their woman pregnant." We all laughed.

"Don't tell Daddy," I told her.

"That's your decision. You know he's going to act the fool, but he has no room to speak on anyone's situation," she stated.

"What's going on?" I asked.

She shook her head. "He says, he's in love with us both." I can't believe my daddy is doing this. That woman is no good for him. If a woman can boldly lay down with another woman's husband, she ain't worth shit.

"I can't believe him," I said shaking my head. "You and Love can stay with me."

She shook her head no. "Love wants to stay with you until I find a place for us to move. I'll be staying with my sister until I do." I pleaded with her to move with me, but she declined. I was ecstatic about having Love staying with me . I gave myself a mental note to visit my dad.

Fila

"Shit! What time is it?" Paisley asked sitting up in the bed. She started searching for her phone as I sat up in the bed watching television. "Why are you just sitting there? What time is it?" She threw a pillow at me.

I laughed. She looked so damn cute with her big afro. I remembered pulling out her ponytail holder when she was sliding my dick inside her mouth. "What time you gotta be to work?"

"Eleven," she said pulling her uniform out the closet.

"Paisley, it's almost three o'clock," I said smiling at her.

"Ugh!" She screamed in frustration. "Why didn't you wake me up?" Everything about her chocolate body was perfect. I could feel my dick getting hard as I watched her scramble around the room in her birthday suit.

"I didn't know you had to work," I said flipping the channels. She finally found her phone and called her job. She made up a lie about having a family emergency. When she got off the phone, she calmed down.

A Love Worth the Fight 3   Nona Day

"Come here," I said staring at her. She rolled her eyes and walked to my side of the bed. I pulled her down on my lap and she straddled me.

"You with me?" I asked staring at her.

"Yes," she replied softly.

"Let the jobs go and follow your dreams Paisley. Stop procrastinating because of fear. I got you," I told her.

"I don't want to rely on you to pay my bills Fila. That's not why I'm with you," she said.

"I know, but when will you ever be able to do what you want if you slaving for someone else?" I asked her.

"I have been thinking about applying for a small business loan. I have great credit. I just need help putting together a business plan," she informed me.

"Make it happen. I'm sure Sheba can help you with that."

A smile appeared on her face. "Ok."

"Now, get dressed. We are meeting your father for a late lunch," I said smiling at her. Her eyes grew big. "He came by, but you were sleep."

"You answered my door?" She asked in disbelief.

I laughed. "Yeah . We talked. I explained everything to him. He wasn't happy about the situation, but he knows how I feel about you."

Before she could reply my phone rang. I looked at the screen to see who was calling. It was the nurse I was paying to give me information on Travis. "The cop just left. If you wanna see him, now is a good time to come," she said when I answered.

"Be there in thirty minutes," I said ending the call.

Paisley gave me a puzzled look. "That was my dad?"

"Nah, I gotta go handle some business. I'll meet you at the restaurant as soon as I'm done. He's expecting you at four o'clock."

"What's going on? I see that look in your eyes Fila."

"Let me handle business. I got this. I just need you to handle my personal shit," I said massaging her thighs.

"What personal shit?" She asked. I looked down at my brick hard dick. She giggled.

"No, because I just realized I'm sore as hell," she said rolling her eyes at me.

I burst into laughter. "Don't blame me because the freak in you came out last night."

"That shit hurts at first, but feels so good once it's in," she said smiling. "But don't be expecting that on the regular. That's only for special occasions."

I laughed. "Well, I guess I'll be getting some more tonight."

"Ain't nothing special about going out to eat with my Daddy," she said getting off my lap. Damn, I wanted slide inside her before I left.

"Look out the window," I told her.

She walked over and looked out the window. She started jumping up and down as she screamed. An all-white Lexus SUV was parked outside with a red bow around it. She rushed putting on clothes and hurried out the door. I followed behind her. I watched her tear the bow off and try to get inside the vehicle. She turned to face me.

"Where are the keys?" She asked anxiously.

"What do I get if I give them to you?" I asked, taunting her.

She slapped me on the arm. "Stop playing boy and give me the keys." I laughed because she was dead serious. I handed her the keys. She wasted no time hitting the unlock switch. She was in awe at the inside of the truck. I had custom seat covers made with the letter P on them. Everything was white expect the initials. I had her initial monogramed in her favorite color, burgundy. She turned to face me with tears running down her face.

"I got you for the rest of my life. You didn't have to do this," she said emotionally.

"I know. I wanted to." She threw her arms around my neck giving me a deep passionate kiss. We ended up in the bedroom going at it like animals. We both were running late when we parted ways.

I arrived at the hospital and the nurse showed me to Travis' room. He was asleep when I walked inside. The bruises on his face were still healing. I fucked up his left eye. I know he wouldn't be able to see out of it. I pulled up a chair and sat beside his bed. I guess he felt my presence because he woke up. He looked at me like I was the scariest man on earth. He reached for the button to call the nurse, but I stopped him.

"I'm only here to talk," I said staring at him. He started mumbling. I realized he couldn't talk because his jaw was wired shut. I noticed the pen and paper in his lap. "I'm going to ask you some questions. Write your answers down." He nodded his head in agreement.

"The cops been by here?" I asked. He shook his head no. "Don't lie to me. Your life depends on it." He closed his eyes and took a deep breath. He wrote on the paper that a detective had been by.

"What does he want?" I asked. He wrote "you" on the paper informing me the detective was after me. I went on to ask him several more questions. I got all the information I needed. I told him as soon as they release him from the hospital to leave town. I didn't give a damn where he went as long as he wasn't here. The only reason he's still living is because I would be the first suspect in his murder. I left the hospital with my mind working on ways to destroy the ones trying to bring me down.

Basilio

"**I** know you taught her to shoot a gun," I said to Sheba as we sat in the den. Worth had walked her mother outside to her car. We all sat and ate together. I got to know a lot about Worth listening to her mother. Worth has always been a fighter with a big heart. She loves hard and fights for the ones she loves even harder.

"She wanted to be able to protect herself. I couldn't deny her that," she explained.

"She almost killed me," I told her. Sheba laughed. I shook my head remembering she fired the gun at me. "How was your vacation."

"It was perfect. I couldn't have asked for things to go any better. I just wish you would've came with us," she said sadly.

"We'll plan another one when all this is over, and do it all over again," I said winking at her. She smiled.

"I can't believe you killed Sanchez. That was a dangerous move," she said in a low voice.

I shrugged my shoulders. "I had nothing to lose. It was him or me."

"So, what now?" She asked. "Dose told me you have eyes on you."

"Yeah , that's why I told you to park in the garage. I'm not supposed to be near her. All this time we thought Moreno was running shit. He was just a face. His sister, Camila runs shit. I can tell the bitch has ice water running through her veins. She will kill her own brother for a dollar. My plan is to turn him against her. I need to know who's the head of all the cartels. That is the key to walking away with our lives."

"And you think we can make him do that?" She asked. I nodded my head yes.

"I have to bring in three new family members. We're meeting at the club in a couple of hours. I'm going to slip out with you in your car. I was able to lose them last night in Dose's car. He dropped me off here."

"And if he doesn't turn on her?" She asked.

I shrugged my shoulders. "I'm in this game for life." I saw a sadness come over my twin sister's face. She wanted me to have what I never thought was for me. She knew I would never bring Worth into this life knowing how my mother died. We stopped talking when Worth walked back into the den.

"I'm going to clean up the kitchen before I leave," Sheba said standing up.

"You don't have to do that. I'll clean it up," Worth said to her. I sat there staring at her beauty. Her hair was tangled and messy. She wore an oversized tee shirt, tights and slippers on her feet. She still looked like the most beautiful woman on earth to me. I noticed she had gained a few pounds. I wasn't complaining. I love every inch of her thickness.

"No, I got it. You relax," Sheba said walking out the den. Worth nervously walked over to the mini bar.

"You want a drink?" She asked.

"Nah, I want you to come sit with me. I need to talk to you," I said. She walked over and sat on the couch beside me. "Are you okay Bella?"

"Are you leaving again?" She asked staring at me. I hated what I was doing to her. She wasn't sure if we were going to have a life together. I didn't know either, but I was willing to die trying.

"I have a meeting at the club in a couple of hours. I want you to get pretty and go to the club tonight."

She smiled. "Are you coming with me?"

I dropped my head dreading having to explain this to her. I had to tell her the truth for her to believe in me.

"Bella, I'm trying to make things right for us. In order for me to do this, I can't be seen with you right now."

Her emeralds started to sparkle as her face frowned up. "I thought you wasn't going to marry her."

"I'm not Bella. Maria is in a far worse situation than I could ever have imagined for her," I said remembering seeing her working in the fields. "I don't want you living in this corrupt life with me. I'm making moves to walk away. I need for you to be understanding and patient with me."

She stared at me with sad eyes. "What about your father's legacy. I know how much that means to you. I'm willing to live any life with you. I know you will protect me."

"I have lived his legacy, now it's time to build mine with you," I said. "Bella, I need you to always be aware of your surroundings. Someone will have eyes on you at all times."

"Am I in danger?" She asked worriedly.

"Not as long as you stay away from me." She gave me a harsh look. "We will spend time together. We just can't be seen in public."

"Why?"

"They feel like you are a distraction for me," I confessed to her.

"I am?"

I chuckled. "A beautiful delight you are, but no distraction. She smiled. "I have to get ready to go to the club. You want to shower with me?"

A big grin came across her face. "Race you upstairs." She took off running toward the stairs. I caught up with her and threw her over my shoulders. We fucked each other until we were breathless. I dressed while she lounged on the bed talking to me. Sheba knocked on the door interrupting our conversation. Worth told her to come in.

"I'll be waiting in the garage for you. Worth, I'll see you at the club later," she said smiling at Worth.

After we left, Sheba went back to her house to make it seem like she was picking me up. I was laid down in the back seat. Once she entered her garage, we went inside the house. Dose was waiting for me, so we could drive to the club. Dose and I went straight to the office once we made it to the club. I poured myself a drink and waited for our three new business partners. It didn't take long for the knock on the door. One of the bartenders opened the door letting us know our guest had arrived. He opened the door wider and in walked Orpheus, Max and Damien. Damien was a young hustler from Georgia. I was his connect and watched how he grew his team over the two years we've been doing business. He was also into smuggling weapons. I've purchased several from him. He was silent and deadly. I wanted Riley in on the deal, but I knew he was trying to get out the life like I was. I didn't want to chance him getting sucked deeper in if this plan doesn't work. We all greeted each other and had a seat at the round table in the office.

"Who this nigga?" Max asked staring at Damien. Damien stared him down without cracking a smile. I know these two will bump heads. Max loves talking shit and Damien doesn't like hearing bullshit .

"Ask yo mama?" Damien replied staring at him.

Max laughed. "Damn nigga you sound like that old ass singer Barry White with that deep ass voice. Sang Secret Garden for us. I bet you can nail that shit." I tried not to laugh but I couldn't help it. Max was always clowning.

"Fuck you nigga," Damien said laughing with us. I stood up when I heard a knock on the door. I looked at the security monitor to see who it was. I was almost knocked off my feet to see Camila standing on the other side of the door. She wasn't even supposed to know about this meeting.

Worth

After Basilio and Sheba left, I called to make sure Love was okay. Our father was her heart. He could do no wrong in her eyes. I know this had to be hard on her. She was doing makeup and said she would be here later tonight. I had already given her a key to the house. I told her to let herself in, since I won't be there. I promised her we would spend the day together tomorrow with Mommy. Our mother seemed okay with her decision. I thought she would be crying and depressed after leaving our father, but she wasn't. She said she did all the crying and doing the self-pity thing while making her mind up to leave him. Now, she wants to move on with her life and live again. As much as I hated to see their marriage end, it felt good seeing her acting like her old self.

I had changed into five different outfits. I could see the weight gain in everything I put on. Black is slimming, so I decided on a black contour, low cut body dress. Even though I had gained a few pounds, I smiled at all my thickness as I gave myself a once over. I hadn't started showing yet, because I already had a little pouch in my stomach. I wanted to tell Basilio about the baby, but I couldn't bring myself to do it. After hearing everything he said, I knew him finding out I was pregnant would be a distraction. I wanted him to focus on what needs to be done. I'll take care of me and our baby until he's done. I blow dried and flat ironed my hair. I decided to wear it bone straight. I slipped on a pair of stilettos and applied a small amount of makeup. I answered my phone when it rang.

"I'm outside," Paisley said when I answered.

"Coming," I said grabbing my clutch. I made sure to lock up before leaving. I smiled when I saw the beautiful Lexus SUV Fila bought her.

"Somebody getting thicker in all the right places. Shit, I need to get pregnant," she said when I hopped in truck.

I laughed. "Is it that obvious?" I didn't want people to start asking me about my weight gain.

"Nah, just look like happy fat," she said smiling.

"What the hell is happy fat?" I asked laughing.

"You know that weight gain where you in love, getting fucked and eaten good, nigga taking you out to eat on the regular, telling you how much he love you, being faithful and loyal. You know all that good shit us women crave from our man." I laughed as she ran down her list.

"Well bitch, you should be a cow then. Got that man outchea buying you a hundred thousand dollar truck and shit," I said laughing.

"Girl, I could eat a cow and my lil ass still won't gain any weight," she said. I laughed.

"I love it. I'm so happy you guys worked things out," I told her.

"It's still a lot he has to deal with. She's not going to let him go easily. Only difference now is I'm not walking away without a fight," she said smiling at me.

"Good."

"Bitch, I'm gone need you to put that damn gun away. You fucking trigger happy. Sheba told me you almost killed Basilio," she said glancing at me as she drove.

I giggled. "I grazed his arm. That is far from almost killing him." She shook her head. "Why you never told me how powerful it feels to shoot one?"

"Worth, lock the gun in a safe please," she said with a serious face.

"I didn't have a choice. He took it from me," I said sadly. She laughed.

"Jesus, why is the club so packed?" Paisley asked when we pulled up to valet parking.

"Somebody must be having a party or something," I said before exiting the vehicle. We made our way to the entrance. "Somebody having a party?" I asked the bouncer.

"Yeah , a nigga named Tree," he answered.

"Who is that?" Paisley asked as we made our way to VIP.

"Some obnoxious asshole Nika fucking with," I told her. Once we were in the VIP, we started looking for a table. It was so crowded I didn't know if we would be able to get one.

"Damn, I was wondering were y'all coming," Sheba said walking up to us. "Follow me." We did as she instructed. We had a table set up with expensive wine and liquor. I hated I couldn't drink.

"Hope you can handle Elsa," Paisley said looking at me. I gave her a confused look. "My truck, because you are my DD tonight." I laughed.

The moment we sat down, I spotted Basilio's table. There were several people around the table. I recognized Max from Vegas, Fila and Dose. I didn't know who the other two guys were. He saw me staring at him and winked at me. I couldn't help but blush. My blushing immediately went away when I noticed a beautiful woman walk over and take a seat at the table. She placed her hand on his thigh and whispered in his ear. My blood started to boil. I relaxed when he moved her hand from his thigh. He said something to her. I could tell by her facial expression she didn't like what he said. I wondered who she was. I had to remember everything he told me, so I stopped staring in their direction. Fila walked over and greeted Paisley with a kiss. I spoke giving him a hug. The most annoying thing about being pregnant was frequent trips to the bathroom.

"I'm going to the bathroom," I told Paisley as she flirted with Fila. She offered to go with me, but I told her to stay at the table.

When I entered the bathroom, I started to turn around when I saw Nika. I changed my mind when I noticed she was crying. I took a deep breath and walked over to the sofa. I sat beside her. Regardless of what she did, my heart wouldn't let me be cruel toward her. She looked up and immediately started wiping her tears. "What do you want?" She asked with an attitude.

"What are you crying for?" I asked.

"Why do you care?"

I laughed. "You fucked your best friend's man. Then tried to help your other man steal from my new man and you got an attitude with me?"

"Fuck you Worth," she said.

"Fine, sit here and cry by your damn self," I said standing up. I started walking toward one of the stalls.

"He won't let me see her. I know I've been a bad mother lately. I wasn't even the best mother, but I love my daughter. I want to be in her life. I'm trying to get my shit together, but no one will give me a chance." I immediately felt sorry for her. I walked over and sat back down beside her.

"Why won't he let you see her?"

"He says I'm not consistent. He doesn't want me in and out of her life. I'm not going to do it this time. I promise. Her birthday is next week. He won't even let me come to her party," she said as she started back crying. I understood what Lamar was saying but he needs to understand he's only hurting baby Gladys.

"I'll talk to him. Give me your phone number, so I can contact you with the details of the party." I already knew about the party. I just wanted to make sure I can convince Lamar to let her come. She recited her phone number and I put it in my phone.

"Thank you," she said graciously.

"So, this yo man's party?" I asked.

She rolled her eyes. "That's everybody's man." I couldn't understand for the life of me why she chose to be with these kinds of men. She goes from one right to another one knowing they are the same.

"Nika, why you keep doing this to yourself? You deserve better than this."

"He really does like me Worth. He does what I do to him," she said.

"What?" I asked confused.

"We started out in a fucked up way, I'll admit. Then we started really feeling each other, until I found out he was still fucking with his ex-girlfriend. So, I started showing him how to really play the game. Once he seen what I was doing, he started showing me he was the coach and I was only a player in the game," she said with a smirk.

"So, you just gone keep playing the game with him?" I asked.

"What am I supposed to do?" She asked.

"Walk away Nika. If he's feeling you like you are him, he'll stop what he's doing. You need to stop thinking laying with a man validates you. God, you are so beautiful and don't see what I see when I look at you. You have so much more to offer a man than just flesh."

She burst into a deep sob. I held her until she stopped crying. "I'm sorry. I know I said it before, but I truly mean it this time Worth. I know we can never have what we had before. I just want your forgiveness. I want to see you get the happiness you deserve."

"I forgave you a long time ago Nika. And I want the same happiness for you."

"I'm going to get out of here and go home. I have to work in the morning anyway. I'm trying to become manager. I'm getting ready to enroll in school," she said standing up. I smiled at her. It was good seeing her wanting more for herself.

"You staying with your dad?" I asked.

"Yeah , he's never there, so I pretty much have the place to myself," she replied. She turned to walk away.

"Nika," I called her name. She turned to face me. "If you ever need someone to talk to, I'm willing to listen. I'll call you soon as I talk to Lamar."

"Thanks Worth," she said walking out the door. I hurried to the stall and relieved myself.

Paisley

"I think things went well with my dad," I told Fila as we sat to the table at the club. I was nervous about things, but I knew he saw Fila at the game with another woman. I was sleeping so hard that morning, I never knew Fila had left my apartment. He said when my dad showed up, they sat down and talked about his situation. After they were done talking, they went and picked up my vehicle. My only concern now was telling Ma about my relationship with Fila and Dad. I had decided to visit her tomorrow to let her know. I know it wasn't going to go well.

"I knew they would. You coming home with me tonight," he said.

"I can't. I drove," I told him.

"Worth can drive it home. I know she's sober," he said sliding his hand between my thighs.

"Stop it," I said trying to move his hand. It wasn't that it didn't feel good against my skin . The problem was it felt too damn good.

"You shouldn't have worn this short ass dress," he said kissing on my neck while sliding his hand further up my thigh. He pushed my thong to the side and slid his finger between my lower lips. He started stroking my wet pussy and it felt too good to stop him.

"Open your legs wider," he whispered in my ear. I did as he said. I rested my elbow on the table and leaned forward. I looked like I was looking at my phone that was laying on the table. His fingers stroked up and down, round and round my drenched pussy until my clit was throbbing.

"Fila, you gone make me come," I said glancing at him.

"That's the goal," he said gently biting my earlobe. He slid two fingers inside me and pressed his thumb against my swollen clit. I folded my lips inside my mouth to keep from moaning out loud . It was so loud in the club no one would hear me. I just didn't want to draw any more attention to us. If anyone was looking I'm sure they knew what was going on. At this moment, I didn't give a damn. It felt too good to stop. I tried to control my quaking body as I exploded on his hand.

"That's my girl," he said pulling his fingers out of me. I looked down to see my creamy liquid coating his fingers. He slipped his fingers inside his mouth and sucked them clean. He leaned forward covering my mouth with his. I could taste myself when he slid his tongue inside my mouth. I was so caught up in our kiss I could've fucked him right there and not care who saw it.

"We'll finish at home," he said after breaking our kiss.

I smiled at him. "I have to go to the bathroom. I feel nasty sitting here."

"I like nasty," he said winking at me. I went to the bar where Worth and Sheba were talking. I asked Sheba could I use her office bathroom. They both smiled at me. "What?"

"We saw y'all. Y'all nasty," Worth said smiling at me. I covered my face with my hands. Sheba laughed and gave me the code to get into her office. We hurried to her office to freshen up. After checking my makeup and applying some lip gloss, I left the office. I was reading a text from Ced when I bumped into someone. I looked up to see Estelle standing there staring at me with a smirk on her face. Some female that I didn't know was standing beside her.

"You need to watch where you're going," she said staring at me with her hand on her hip. I shook my head and tried to walk past them. She stepped in my way and bumped me causing me to stumble backwards. All the thoughts of her sending her brother to me crossed my mind.

I hated the way she was using her son to keep a hold on Fila. Rage took over me when I thought of her preying on my weaknesses and using Fiji to get me to walk away from the man that I loved. I charged toward her and slammed my fist into her face as hard as I could. We started fighting each other. She was windmilling while I was punching her in the face. This was the time I wish I wouldn't have sewn tracks into my hair before coming out tonight. She grabbed a handful of my weave. I wasn't worried about her pulling my hair from my scalp at the time. I kept throwing punches at her until we stumbled to the floor. I was on top of her still hitting her as she kept a grip on my hair. I felt someone hitting me in the back of my head. I knew it was her friend trying to help her.

"Bitch, get off her!" I heard Worth scream. I didn't feel the girl hitting me anymore. I'm glad I did a rush job on my sew-in . My braids were loose on my scalp. The tugging on my weave wasn't pulling my hair from my scalp. Estelle started screaming for me to get off her. I kept hitting her ass hard as I could. I saw blood coming from her mouth. My face was burning, so I knew she was scratching me. Someone finally pulled me off of her. She kicked me when I was lifted up.

"What the fuck you doing Paisley?" Fila asked holding me in a bear hug.

"That bitch tried me," I yelled trying to get out his grip. A bouncer was helping Estelle off the floor. Her nose and mouth was bleeding. "You better get the bitch before I kill her trifling ass."

"Nigga, you ain't shit! You gone choose pussy over your own son," she said staring at Fila.

"Hold her," he said letting me go. A tall slender guy held me to keep me from beating on Estelle some more. Fila walked over and yoked Estelle up by her neck. I don't know what he said to her, but she calmed her ass down. He let her neck go and grabbed her by the arm.

"Take these bitches out of here," he said shoving her into one of the bouncer's chest.

Basilio

I was trying to make my way through the crowd to see what all the commotion was. Before I could see what was going on I saw one of the bouncers man handling Worth. On instinct I pulled my gun. I was ready to dead the nigga until I heard Sheba's voice. "Watch how you handle her. She's pregnant." Everyone in the club vanished and my eyes zoomed in on Worth. I guess she felt my eyes on her because she turned to look at me. Her eyes were filled with fear and sadness. I pushed my way through the crowd.

"Take her to the office," I told Sheba. I gave Worth a quick glance to make sure she was okay. I walked over to Fila to check to see what was going on. Tree was holding on to Paisley as Fila stood there with his hands around Estelle's neck. The nigga looked like he was going to kill her in the club in front of everybody. I exhaled when he let her go. After he dismissed her, he turned to check on Paisley. I realized Paisley and Worth had to be fighting Estelle and her friend. I walked over to Fila.

"You straight?" I asked.

"Yeah , we bout to get up outta here," he said not taking his hands off Paisley. I saw a few scratches in her face. It was obvious who got their ass beat. Estelle was bleeding from the nose and mouth. Her friend had a busted lip.

I looked at Paisley. "You good?"

"Yeah , you should be asking his bitch ass baby mama that," she said rolling her big pretty eyes at Fila. It was going to be a long night for him.

I almost forgot Camila was in the club. After I turned down her offer to fuck, she turned her attention to Orpheus. I found out tonight that he eloped with Max's sister in law. He had no interest in Camila but decided to entertain her. It didn't take long before she was feeling the drinks he was giving her. I walked back over to the table to see if she heard what Sheba said. Orpheus smiled and winked at me. She could barely hold her head up she was so drunk.

"Y'all might wanna get yo boss lady home. Looks like she can't handle her liquor," I said to her bodyguards . Orpheus helped her stand up.

"I owe you for that one," I whispered to him.

He shrugged his shoulders. "She said she could handle her liquor. We have determined that is a lie." I laughed.

A Love Worth the Fight 3   Nona Day

We never had a chance to sit down and strategize how we were going to move her out of her position. Before I let her into the office, I set up a meeting with them at Sheba and Dose's house for tomorrow. Camila came in giving orders about how she wanted everything ran. We all sat listening to her with no intentions of obeying her orders. I knew her true reasons for coming was to check up on me. Once her security escorted her out the door, I made my way to the office.

"Where's Sheba?" I asked Dose walking up to him.

"She's still in the office with Worth," he said. I walked away ready to get some answers. Sheba was sitting on the sofa beside Worth, who looked like a scared little child.

"Still keeping secrets from me I see," I said staring at Sheba.

She stood up. "It wasn't my secret to tell, Bull." She walked out the office leaving me standing there looking down at Worth. She kept her head down twiddling her fingers.

"You carrying my child?" I asked her. She looked up at me and nodded her head yes. My blood started warming in my veins.

"You are carrying my life inside you and didn't tell me?" She put her head back down. "Look at me!" I mistakenly yelled at her. She jumped and looked at me. I expected to see the scared little girl I saw when I walked in, but she flipped into the fiery Worth. The emerald in her eyes were sparkling.

She jumped up and pushed me in the chest. "Yes, I'm pregnant! No, I didn't tell you! I didn't tell you because you were leaving me to marry another woman. I wasn't going to force you to stay here because I was pregnant!"

"I'm here now! You still didn't tell me! What were you going to do with our child, Worth?" I asked hoping what I was thinking was not an option she was considering.

"I was going to raise my child without you, since you felt running a drug empire is more important than living a life with me." Those words stung. I took a deep breath to calm down.

"I didn't leave for a drug empire. I left because I didn't want your life tainted with my corrupt life. You deserve so much more than that. I watched my mother get gunned down because of the life my father lived. Yes, he loved and tried to protect her with his life. Living the life, I live I can't guarantee your protection. I don't want my life to be the reason yours is ruined."

A Love Worth the Fight 3   Nona Day

"Your life is my life," she said staring at me with her beautiful eyes. "I wanted to tell you when you came back. You started talking about distractions and staying focused. I decided it was best to wait until all that was over."

I chuckled. "And how were you going to keep a baby growing inside you from me?" She shrugged her shoulders. "Come here." She walked over to me. I pulled her in my arms as she rested her head on my chest.

"I promise you we will have our life together," I told her. She pulled away from me.

"Who is that woman?" She asked with an attitude.

It was always funny to me how quick her moods change. "She's the one holding all the cards right now."

"She wants to keep you from me because she wants to fuck you," she said staring at me as if I was guilty of something.

I laughed and sat on the sofa. I couldn't argue with her comment because there was some truth to it. I stared at her round ass in the black dress. Her full breast were nearly pouring out of it. I licked my lips as I thought of sliding inside her. She walked over and stood in front of me. She raised her dress up over her hips revealing her black thong. Her fat juicy mound caused my dick to jump. I unfastened my trousers and she slipped out her thong. My brick hard dick jumped from my boxers like a jack in the box. She straddled my lap and slid her warm, wet tight pussy down on me. I wasted no time pulling her dress completely off. I wanted to lick and suck on her succulent breasts as she slid on my pole. I pushed them together lapping my tongue from one to the other while she was grinding on my dick. I was biting and sucking her hard nipples as she moaned. She lifted up and planted the soles of her feet into the sofa. I lost all train of thought when she started bouncing up and down on me. Her gushing wetness was spilling from her as my dick slid in and out of her. Her breasts were bouncing up and down.

"Fuck!" I groaned slapping her ass as her tight tunnel gripped my shaft. I knew she was getting ready to explode. I gripped her waist and lifted up ramming the head of my dick against her sensitive spot.

"Ssssshhhit I'm cooommming!" She wailed as her body stiffened and trembled. I could feel her thick cream saturating my dick. My dick started spreading inside her. She hopped out of my lap and dropped to her knees. I let out a loud groan when she sucked me into her mouth. She moaned, licked, and slurped up, down and all round my dick. With her hand guiding her mouth I couldn't hold it any longer. I was just about to come when she stopped. If I didn't love her so damn much, I would've choked her to death. She stood up and wiped her mouth with the back of her hand. She stared down at me as I stared up at her like she had lost her damn mind . If I didn't get this nut off, I knew I was going to have blue balls in the morning.

"Don't ever call me Worth again. I am and always will be Bella to you." I had no idea I called her Worth while we were arguing. She picked up her dress and turned to walk in the bathroom. She didn't make it far before I snatched her up. She laughed as I grabbed her around the waist. We sexed each other on the couch, desk, table and floor. When we were done our bodies were dripping wet.

"How are we going to get out of here?" She asked thinking about the fact I'm supposed to stay away from her.

"We are going to get in my car and go home. No more hiding," I said as she lay on top of me on the floor. She looked up at me and smiled.

Fila

Estelle was blowing my phone up after I left the club with Paisley. She hadn't said a word since we got in the car. I knew she was mad as hell. I decided to remain quiet until we made it to my house. I thought she was going to start tripping when she realized I wasn't taking her home. I was taking her to my place. I had purchased a new home that I planned to move into in a couple of weeks. I didn't like the fact that Estelle's family knew where I laid my head.

"I don't have anything to sleep in," she said glancing at me.

"You don't need clothes," I said smiling.

"Oh, you ain't getting none. You cutting these tracks out my hair, since you the reason they are literally hanging on by a thread," she said rolling her eyes at me.

I laughed. I reached over and massaged her thigh. "I'm sorry."

She looked at me with her soft eyes. "It's not your fault your baby mama doesn't know how to let go."

"So, why can't I get any?" I asked smiling.

"Because I gotta do my hair over tomorrow. First, I gotta get this shit out," she said raising a track that was barely hanging on.

"I'm not your girlfriend, Paisley. I'm not going to be helping you do your hair."

She looked at me. "You are my boyfriend. That is one of your duties. After I wash and condition it. I need you to grease my scalp." I laughed and shook my head. Honestly, I didn't mind doing those things for her. We would sit, talk and laugh about any and everything.

"You have some clothes from when you stayed here before," I reminded her.

When we made it to my place, she went upstairs to change . I went into the den and flopped down on the sofa. Estelle called my phone again. This time I decided to answer to make sure Fiji was okay. She started cussing me out the minute I answered. I knew he was okay. I hung up and turned it off. Paisley came and sat down on the floor between my legs. She gave me a pair of scissors.

"If you cut my hair, you are no longer my boyfriend," she said looking back at me over her shoulders.

I couldn't believe I was sitting here cutting weave out a female's hair. I would do anything to keep her happy. I just gotta figure out a way to make that possible without losing my son and freedom. I sat and listened to her tell me childhood stories about her dad. She didn't talk much about her mother. I know they had a relationship, I just didn't know how good it was. My mother was coming into town next week. I couldn't wait for her to meet her. She never liked Estelle. Now, I know why. By the time we were done with her hair, the sun was coming up. We both showered and slid into bed.

"I love you," she said resting her head on my chest.

"I know lil nappy head girl," I said playing with her big puff ball. She giggled. We both drifted off to sleep.

I woke up to the smell of food cooking. I went into the bathroom to brush my teeth. I walked downstairs into the kitchen to see her cooking. "Afternoon, sleepy head," she said smiling at me. I walked up to her and kissed her soft lips.

"Sit down and I'll fix your plate," she said. I did as she instructed.

"I gotta dip out in an hour," I told her as she sat the plate in front of me. This was the first time she cooked for me. She was always working or doing hair, so our time together was with Fiji or late at night. She cooked fried fish, cheese grits, coleslaw and hush puppies. "Damn, what I do to deserve all this?"

She smiled. "Just keep loving me and there's more to come."

I looked down at the food then at her. "You ain't trying to root me up, is you?" She started laughing.

"Nigga, you already whipped. What I need to root you for?" She boasted. I could only laugh, but she was telling the truth. Someone started knocking on the door. We looked at each other wondering who was at the door. She stood up to go answer it .

"Stay in here," I said getting up to see who was at the door. I went into the bedroom to retrieve my gun first. I looked at the security monitor to see Detective Bailey standing there with another officer. I knew shit was going from bad to worse. I slipped on some clothes and walked back in the kitchen. I told Paisley to go in the bedroom and get dressed. Honestly, I didn't know if they were here for me or her. Estelle so grimy, they could be here for her.

Worth

This was the love I wanted. I think this was the type of love every woman desired. He has spoiled me ever since I woke up this morning. I was served breakfast in bed. After I was done eating, we relaxed in a long hot bath together. He has been catering to my every need all day. Now, we were lounging in the bedroom. He's massaging, kissing and talking in Spanish to my belly. I felt like a pervert. He was talking to our baby and my panties were becoming soaked from listening to him. As happy as I was at this moment, I couldn't help but to think about our future.

"What's going to happen now?" I asked.

"We're going to get married and raise our child. What do you mean?" He asked looking at me.

"What about the people that don't want you with me? The ones that want you to keep working with them?" He laid back on the bed and pulled me into his arms. I rested my head on his chest.

"No one will keep me from you and my child. Let me worry about that. I don't want you stressing. You have my life inside you."

I smiled looking up at him. "I thought I was your life."

He chuckled. "You are my soul. Without my soul there is no life," he said placing his hand over my belly.

"Can we stay in bed all day?" I asked. I didn't care about anything negative going on the world. This was the life I wanted with the man I love.

"I wish I could, but I have to be at Sheba's house in an hour. Don't you have plans with Love?" He was right. We got home so late last night I didn't get a chance to talk to Love. She stayed here last night. I was going to help her move her clothes from the house today.

"Yeah , I forgot," I said. I wanted this time with Love. I needed to know how she felt about our father cheating. I planned to speak with my father also while we are there. I texted him this morning to make sure he will be there when we came.

"We will go out to a nice restaurant for dinner," he said.

"I get to wear   one of those fancy ass dresses you bought me in Vegas?" I asked excited.

He laughed. "Yes Bella. The limo will arrive at 8:30 to pick us up."

I tried getting out the bed to see which dress I wanted to wear. He gently pulled me back toward him. "I fed you this morning, now I need to eat." I gave him a bashful grin. He positioned me where I was straddling his face. I rode his face until my essence was spilling from the sides of his mouth. We took a shower together and got dressed. I walked him to the front door.

"I'll be back to get dressed. Then, I'm all yours," he said winking at me. I tiptoed and kissed his lips.

I went upstairs to Love's room. She was tying her hair up in a bun. I flopped down on her bed. She glanced over her shoulder at me and shook her head. "What?" I asked.

"You so dick whipped" She said smiling.

"I'm not," I said laughing. I was dick and tongue whipped. I just wasn't ready to have these conversations with my baby sister. I know she's almost grown, but she'll always be a baby to me.

"Worth, your screams echoed all over this enormous ass house. I damn near had an orgasm just from listening to you," she said. I was so embarrassed she heard me having sex.

"We are moving you to the other side of the house," I said getting off the bed.

She laughed. "Did you not hear me? Your moans and screams echo ." She started mocking how I sound. I threw a pillow at her. "Don't worry I put my headphones on."

"Are you okay living here?" I asked her.

She nodded her head yes. "I can't believe Daddy did this to us."

"Love, I know it seems like he did it to us. He did it to our mother. He loves us none the less. I just don't know if him and Mommy still love each other. I just feel like he was a coward. He should've been left if he wasn't happy with her."

"I know she doesn't love him anymore," she said looking at me.

"How do you know?" I asked.

"She's not broken the way you were when Majesty would hurt you. She's okay. She seems happier." I guess when you let go of what is causing you pain, it starts a healing process. I know she may seem fine now but eventually, all that hurt will come to the surface.

"Well, we are going to make sure she stays happy," I told her. "You ready?" We left the house headed over to my father's house.

Our daddy's car was parked in the driveway when we arrived. I used my house key to let us in. Love went to her room to start packing her clothes. "Daddy," I called out his name. It was quiet . No lights were on in the house. I headed down the hall to his bedroom. I knocked on the door, but he didn't answer. I turned the knob and the door opened.

"Daddy!" I screamed as I rushed to him. He was laying on the floor. I tried waking him up but couldn't. Love came rushing in the room. She started crying and trying to wake him up. I called 911. I am angry with him, but I don't want to lose my daddy.

Basilio

"**H**ow does it feel knowing you're going to be a daddy?" Sheba asked as we sat in her den. We were waiting on Fila to arrive. I couldn't stop the big grin from appearing on my face.

"I wanted to tell you, but she pleaded with me not to. It wasn't my place. I'm sorry," she said with regretful eyes.

I nodded my head. "It's cool. We talked it out. I understood why she kept quiet. Shit different now Sheba. There's no negotiating this shit. We all walking out of this life. I know you and Dose are willing to step in and lead the family but it's not going to happen."

She stared at me. "You don't think we can handle it?"

"I know you can. I just want a better life for us. I know Dose will still hustle his territories, but he will be free to do as he chooses . He won't be obligated to anyone but himself. I want you to experience what Worth is feeling now. The joy of having a life growing inside you. I know you will never allow yourself that if you chose to run the families."

Natavia Presents

"How can we walk away from this? As powerful as you are, she has you in a box right now," she asked.

"Everyone has a boss. I just need to know who's her boss. If it was up to her, I would be dead right now. It's not her decision, just like it wasn't Moreno's decision," I told her.

"Hey, Fila said to go ahead. I'll fill him in later. He just said something came up," Dose said shrugging his shoulders. I know Fila is dealing with a lot right now. As soon as we get this shit straight, we'll get his shit straight. I followed Dose to the game room where Max, Orpheus and Damien was waiting.

"I'm not going to keep you here. I know you need to get back to your families," I told them.

"Yeah , we going into the studio ain't that right Barry White?" Max said winking at Damien. "We making a new rendition of Secret Garden. I'm going to be El Debarge and Orpheus gone be Al B. Sure. What y'all think?" We all laughed except Damien. He always kept a mean mug on his face.

"He's annoying as fuck," Damien said shaking his head.

"Yeah , but he is a money hungry hustler and killer just like you," I reminded him. Max nodded his head and winked at Damien agreeing with me.

"Man, y'all country mothafuckas wild as hell. Damn girls fight like dudes down in the dirty south," Max said laughing. "That lil pretty eyed girl might beat yo Sombrero wearing ass. You better watch out."

I just shook my head. "Before we began, I have one question." They all looked at me. "Is this going to cause conflict with your personal lives?"

"I'm good," Damien stated.

"You know I'm straight. Orpheus straight too. His wife lives in the ocean," Max said smiling at Orpheus. Dose and Damien laughed remembering the jokes about his sister in law's big feet.

"I'm good," Orpheus said laughing.

We sat down and told them what territories they will supply. They are taking over all of me, Eduardo and Antonio's territory. All I will be doing is supplying them. I'm hoping this will get me closer to who's over Camila.

"That's a lot of damn money. My damn dick hard right now," Damien said smiling. Max fell out laughing. Everybody looked at him.

"This nigga go from looking like Shrek to a lil school boy when he smiles," he said laughing. He wasn't lying. Whenever Damien smiled he looked innocent as hell.

"Fuck you nigga," Damien said to Max.

"That's the easy part. Here's the hard part. I'm trying to shut down the families. If I succeed, you walk away with all that territory. It's yours to manage as you want. If I don't, you are stuck with the family and rules. I know that doesn't seem hard, but I'm telling you it is if you ever wanna walk away. I'm the most money making man in the family and can't walk away."

"What do you need us to do to help you shut it down?" Orpheus asked.

"Right now, just make as much money as you can. They don't know I'm not going to be supplying customers. I need to be able to show them you can make just as much money as I could. With just me, it takes longer. With three of you, they get faster money. If they are happy with the results, they will supply you. There will be no need for me anymore. First, I gotta get Camila out of the way. She's the one keeping me locked in."

"I can just kill the drunk bitch," Orpheus said shrugging his shoulders.

I chuckled. "Then we'll have a cartel war. I'm trying to walk away with my life."

"So, everybody in?" Dose asked. They all nodded their head yes. We all kicked back and celebrated our new partnership until my phone rang. I rushed out of the house headed to the hospital.

Fila

Paisley didn't ask any questions. She did as I instructed. I opened the door to see Detective Bailey standing there with a smirk on his face. "What the fuck you want?"

He chuckled. "That's negotiable."

"I don't have time for guessing games," I said. I attempted to close the door, but he stopped me by putting his hand up to the door.

"I have reason to believe Paisley Edwards is here. We have a warrant for her arrest. Seems like you two have something in common. She likes beating on people just like you," he said with a smile. All I could think about was killing Estelle's trifling ass. I knew she would do some foul ass shit like this. There was no way I was letting him take her to jail. I stepped outside closing the door behind me.

"What do I have to do to make this go away?" I asked staring at him. I wanted to kill him with my bare hands. I know he was going to dig deep in my pockets. I didn't mind paying for her freedom. I just didn't want to put the money in the grimy crackers pocket. I didn't want her having a criminal record.

He chuckled. "I'm glad you are starting to see things my way. Twenty-thousand will make all this go away." My blood warmed up. "As far as me leaving you alone, that will cost more."

"Dig as much as you want. You won't discover a damn thing. "I'll have your damn money in a couple of hours."

A big smile came across his face. "I'll give you call. When I get the info I want on you, we'll negotiate again." He walked away with the dirty cop behind him. I made sure to get the officers name on his badge. I'm going to make sure both of them are handled.

When I went back in the house, Paisley was sitting there looking nervous. She jumped up looking at me. "What's wrong?"

"Nothing," I said pulling her in my arms. "He was just stopping by to make sure I was abiding by the rules."

"What rules?" She asked.

"He was just making sure I didn't have Fiji over here unsupervised," I lied. She pulled out of my arms and flopped down in the chair.

"I hate this. She's only doing this because you are with me," she said with sad eyes.

"Paisley, don't start tripping. Don't start thinking no bullshit about walking away. I'll fuck yo lil ass up you, start talking crazy." I was dead ass serious. I know that's the shit she was thinking. By any means necessary, I was going to have her and my son with me.

She looked up at me. "I ain't scared of you."

I laughed. "Just because you beat Estelle's ass, don't get it twisted. I'll fold your lil ass up."

She laughed. "When do you get to see Fiji again?"

"Tomorrow, it's one of those supervised visits. Pops keeping him next week, so I'll get to spend some time with him. I figured we could all do something together," I told her. She smiled.

"Damn, let me go eat my food. I gotta get outta here. I got some shit to handle," I told her.

She stood up and pulled me by my arm leading me to the bedroom. "Not until you handle me." Paisley had the kind of sex that made a nigga lose focus. Everything I needed to be doing was pushed to the back of my mind .

When I left my house, her sweaty, chocolate body was spread out over my bed speechless. I met up with Detective Bailey. I knew I couldn't waste time paying him. I wasn't going to risk Paisley's freedom by not paying him.

"I see you cover your tracks well. There's always a slip up. I'll find it, trust me," he said as we stood inside an old abandoned house. It was down a long secluded dirt road. I was familiar with the neighborhood because I've ridden four wheelers in the area numerous times. This was one of the reasons I didn't make a lot of noise in the streets. I handled enemies and business when necessary. When you out here making noise just to be known, you get attention from the wrong people.

I smirked at him. "No slip ups when you are a legit business man. Now that we are done here, I have business to handle."

Estelle had moved back to her house. When I arrived, she was walking inside the house. She didn't have Fiji with her. She knows I didn't like her leaving our son at her mother's house without her there with him. Stella had too many niggas in and out of her house. If one of them causes harm to him, I'll be locked up for the rest of my life. I got out the car and went inside. She was in the kitchen pouring a glass of wine. She turned to face me, and I had to hold my laugh in. Her lip was swollen, and she had a black eye.

"Yo bitch going to jail," she said turning to face me.

"Where's Fiji?" I asked ignoring her statement.

She gulped down the glass of wine. She wasn't supposed to be drinking. "He's with Shawna."

I walked up to her and stared down at her. "When we go to court Tuesday, you will drop this custody battle. I've been playing nice with you . After Tuesday, that changes if you still on bullshit."

"I know you the reason my brother leaving town. You won't run me away," she said.

I chuckled. "Last warning. Drop the charges." I pulled out my phone to make sure Fiji was with Shawna. She answered on the second ring. After speaking to Fiji , he informed me he was having a sleepover at Shawna's house with Pookie. I left Estelle standing there in her own misery. I had plans for her if she didn't do as I say.

Worth

Love and I were a complete mess sitting in the ER's waiting room. I tried not to think the worst , but our father looked so weak. I didn't see the strong, healthy man that I'm used to seeing. I don't know if he had a heart attack or stroke. We were waiting for answers. We had only been there for fifteen minutes, but it felt more like fifteen hours. I wanted a chance to make things right with my dad. Our relationship has been so strained lately. I restricted his attempts to talk and mend our relationship. I'll do anything to have that chance now. I don't want to lose my daddy this soon.

"You think we should call Mommy?" Love said with her red eyes. We both cried holding our dad until the ambulance arrived. My mind was so focused on Daddy until I completely forgot about Mommy. I nodded my head yes to Love. She dialed our mother's phone number. Just as she started talking to our mother, I was distracted by Basilio coming through the ER's doors. I walked over to him.

"What's going on?" He asked looking me over to make sure I was okay.

"It's our father. We found him barely breathing on the bedroom floor. We're waiting for someone to come tell us what's wrong with him." He pulled me into his arms and held me tight as I started to cry. The thought of my dad dying was too much to bear.

"He's going to be okay, Bella," he whispered in my ear.

"Our father is a very fit man. He takes care of his health. I don't know how he could have a heart attack or stroke," I told him.

"Let's wait and talk to the doctor. It might not be anything serious," he said. As much as I wanted to believe him, I couldn't. I could tell our father was fighting for his life.

About thirty minutes later, our mother came through the ER's doors. I could see the worry and fear in her face. She hugged me and Love tight. We all sat back down and quietly waited for some answers. Not long after, a young white doctor walked up to us. "The Plenty family?" He asked glancing at all of us. Mommy nodded her head yes. I had a death grip on Basilio's hand praying he didn't say my daddy was dead.

"It was rough, but we have him stable. He had a sudden cardiac arrest. He's very weak right now. We had to put a stint in his heart because only thirty percent was working. He should make a full recovery with a proper diet and exercise," he informed us.

"Can we see him?" Love asked anxiously.

"They are moving him to the ICU floor. We will keep him there for a few days. You will be able to visit him two at a time once he is settled in. A nurse will come get you as soon as he's in his room."

We all breathed a sigh of relief. "Thank you," Mommy said to the doctor.

While we waited to see Daddy, I realized I hadn't eaten since this morning. My stomach was starting to growl. I was going to ask Basilio to grab me something from the cafeteria, but the nurse came to let us know we could see Daddy. We followed her to the third floor. I told Mommy and Love to go in and see him first. I sat with Basilio thankful that my daddy was still here.

"You don't have to stay. I know you have a lot going on," I said looking at Basilio. He looked at me as if I had grown a second head.

"Bella, nothing comes before you." I smiled and kissed his soft lips.

About thirty minutes later, Mommy and Love came out and said Daddy wanted to speak with me alone. I was anxious to talk to him. I wanted to apologize for trying to shut him out my life. Regardless of what he was doing in his marriage, he was always a good daddy. It broke my heart to see him hooked to so many machines when I walked in the room. I was still thankful he was alive. He was barely conscious. He instructed me to come closer in his weak froggy voice.

"Daddy, you don't have to talk. You need to rest," I told him holding his hand. He mumbled. I heard his words but wanted to be sure I heard correctly.

"What?" I asked.

"Get away from that man. He's dangerous," he mumbled with a tired voice.

"Who?" I asked. The only man my daddy didn't like is Majesty and he is dead.

"Bull, he's involved with some dangerous people. They tried to kill me," he said. My heart started beating rapidly.

"Daddy, he wouldn't hurt you," I assured him. He tried to speak but the monitor started going haywire. The nurses ordered me to leave the room to work on him. I rushed out the room. I didn't understand what was going on, but I was furious and scared to death. My family's life was in danger.

I stood there staring at Basilio. "They tried to kill him. You said you would protect me. That included my family too." Tears started to fall from my eyes. I was the reason my father almost died.

"Bella, what…" were the only words I let come out his mouth.

"Get out! You can't be here!" I screamed at him. He stepped back from me. My mother rushed to me to calm me down.

"What's going on?" She asked.

"Just make him leave. He has to go. He can't be here with me," I said turning away from him.

"I don't know what's going on, but I think it's best for now, Bull," Mommy told him.

"Bella, I will go but I'm not walking away from you and my child," he said. I felt his presence walk away. Reality hit me as to how dangerous his life is. I was willing to risk my own life for him but not the life of my family.

Paisley

"**B**itch, you must have lost your damn mind," I said to Estelle when I opened my door. I can't believe she had the nerve to show up at my apartment. I was trying to finish my hair, so I could visit my mother. That was a visit I was dreading. I didn't have the patience or nerves to deal with Estelle.

"It's in your best interest to let me in," she said.

I laughed. "You know I have the right to whoop your ass inside my apartment, right?"

She rolled her eyes. "Fila might've paid for your freedom but what I have on him you can't afford to let me walk away from this door." I had no idea what she meant by Fila paying for my freedom. That wasn't my concern at the time. I wanted to know what she had on Fila. I didn't trust the bitch.

"I'm not letting you inside my apartment," I told her. I stepped outside. "What is it?"

She held up a flip phone. I knew it was a TracFone. "He slipped up. I found it in the sofa when I was cleaning. There's enough information in this phone to send him away for a very long time."

I laughed. "You expect me to believe that? I don't know what's in that phone." Even though I was trying to call her bluff, I was nervous as hell. She flipped the phone open to show me messages between Fila and Majesty. It spoke of a murder they committed about a year ago. I knew it was true, because I remembered the turf war they were having with the guy they killed. My heart dropped. I had to get the phone away from her.

"Before you even think about trying to take this phone from me, I have screen shots of this conversation," she said. She read my mind.

"What do you want?" I asked feeling defeated.

"I want you to leave town like he's making my brother leave town. You are supposed to be locked up now. He paid for your freedom. Now, you will pay for his freedom," she said with a smirk. Before I knew it, I had slapped the taste out of her mouth. She fell to the ground. I was going to beat her senseless until I saw my brother pull into a parking space. She got up off the ground wiping the blood from her mouth. I realized beating this bitch wasn't going to stop her. She was determined to get me out of Fila's life.

"You have five days to get out of town. If you are still here, I'm turning this information in. If you tell Fila, he will be locked up for murder," she said with cold eyes.

"It doesn't matter if I'm here or not. He doesn't want you anymore," I told her.

"Do what I said," she said before walking off. I wasn't falling for her trap twice. I was going to tell Fila what she has on him.

"Damn, who was that? You slapped the dog shit out of her," Ced said walking up to me.

"Fila's delusional ass ex-fiancé," I said turning to walk back into the apartment. I went straight for my phone. I kept trying to call Fila, but he wouldn't answer. I sent him a text letting him know I needed to speak to him ASAP.

"You straight?" He asked me with concern in his eyes.

"Yeah , I'm good. She just gets under my damn skin," I lied. "What brings you by?" I asked.

"I came by to see if you had any update on Love's dad. She told me he was rushed to the ER. I've been trying to call her ever since. She keeps sending me to voicemail." I panicked. I know Worth had to be a mess right now. I immediately started looking for my keys.

A Love Worth the Fight 3   Nona Day

"I didn't know anything about this. I haven't talked to Worth today," I said steadily searching for my keys.

"Paisley, calm down. You ain't in no shape to drive anyway. I'll take you," he said. I didn't have time to argue with him. I grabbed my purse and rushed out the door.

When we arrived at the hospital. Love was sitting there looking tired and scared. I walked over and hugged her tight. She rolled her eyes at Ced. He didn't say anything to her. I would ask him about that later. Love informed me Worth and her mother was in the room with her father. I sat with Love and she told me everything that happened. She said Bull had left only minutes before we showed up. She had no idea what was going on. I wasn't exactly sure. All I know is Bull was going to make someone pay for Worth's father being in the hospital. Since Fila hadn't returned my call or text, I called Sheba.

"It's a storm coming. Make sure all the animals are calm," I said to her. Lately Sheba has been teaching Worth and I how to talk in codes. Animal was a reference to Bull. She didn't reply. She hung up the phone. I sat and waited until I could speak with Worth. I know she had to be going crazy.

Fila

"Who is it?" the woman said on the other side of the door.

I cleared my throat. "Fila." She snatched the door open and stared me down from head to toe through her screen door.

"Nigga, I don't know you. My cougar days are over. You a couple years too late. You fine as hell though. Who you?" She asked giving me a seductive stare. She is a beautiful woman. I could see her looking just like Paisley in her younger days.

"I was wondering if I could have a word with you. I'm a friend of your daughter." She stared at me with worry in her eyes. "She's okay. There's absolutely nothing wrong with her."

"There has to be something if you showing up at my residence ," she said.

"Can I come in?" I asked. She cautiously unlocked the screen door. I stepped inside her apartment. I was shocked to see how nice the place was. She had some stylish and expensive furniture and decorations in the tiny apartment.

"Surprised to see somebody living in the projects with nice shit?" She asked as I looked around. I gave her a half smile. "Come in and sit down. Don't be trying to scope my place out. I have a gun. I will kill a mothafucka trying to rob me." I chuckled.

"You don't have to worry about that," I assured her. She nodded her head.

"How you know my baby?" She asked.

I didn't know how this was going to go. I had a long talk with Paisley's dad. He filled me in on the history of their relationship. I understood why Paisley never mentioned her mom. She doesn't think she would approve of her seeing me. I decided to take it upon myself to discuss it with her. I wasn't going to mention Paisley reconnected with her dad. I would leave that up to Paisley. I just wanted Paisley to feel free to love me. I can tell there's still doubt in her heart about us.

"We've been dating for a while now," I confessed.

She squinted her eyes and stared at me. "You that got damn married man, ain't you?"

"Nah, I was never married," I told her.

"You got a fiancé," she said.

I took a deep breath. "I had one, but that's over." I have killed some of the scariest looking niggas in the world. My heart never skipped a beat. For some reason she made me nervous. I don't think Paisley would feel comfortable being with me without her mother's approval.

"So, you left her to be with my daughter. I didn't raise my daughter to be a home wrecker. You will not bring that bad name on my baby. I may not have been the best mother at times, but I raised her to be a respectful young lady. I didn't raise her to fuck another woman's man." She was furious.

"Where my damn phone?" She yelled looking around. "I'm bout to give that lil heifer a piece of my mind. I told her to leave yo ass alone. She had a nice young man trying to date her. I guess she was too busy fucking somebody's man to give him a chance." She grabbed her phone.

I blurted the words out before I knew it. "That nigga tried to rape her." She froze and stared at me. I knew I was wrong for saying it, but I still wanted to kill the nigga for putting his hands on her. I ran my hands over the top of my head trying to get the image of her bruised face out of my head.

"What?" She asked with tears in her eyes. I assured her Paisley was okay and wasn't hurt. She breathed a sigh

Natavia Presents

of relief. I could tell she loved her daughter. I didn't have a choice but to tell her what happen.

"Why are you here?" She asked.

"I love your daughter. Paisley didn't break up a happy home. Our relationship was over before we became involved. Right now, she's scared to tell you about us. All I'm asking for is a chance to show you that I can make your daughter happy."

"So, you just gone walk away from yo child?" She asked with disgust.

"My son comes before anyone, even Paisley. She knows that. She would walk away from me if she felt like she was to blame for me not being with my son. I will always be a father to my child."

She sat quietly. "And if the child's mother doesn't want her son around Paisley?"

I stared her in the eyes. "What kind of woman would keep her child from his father because he doesn't want her anymore?" I wanted her to realize what she did to Paisley keeping her from her father. I saw the shame in her eyes. She stood up and walked away. I assumed she went into the bathroom. She came back into the living room a few minutes later.

"Thank you for coming by. I will talk with my daughter," she said looking down at me. I didn't know if that was a bad or good thing. I stood up and walked to the door. I felt her presence walking behind me.

"Nigga, if you hurt my daughter I will cut your dick off and shove it up your ass," she said when I turned to face her. I almost burst out laughing. I saw the seriousness in her face and held it in. I simply nodded my head.

When I got in the car, I realized I had several missed calls and texts from Paisley. I knew something was wrong. Her last text told me to meet her at the hospital. I couldn't get there fast enough. When I arrived, I was relieved to see her sitting and talking with Worth. Worth's eyes were bloodshot red. She looked as if she had the weight of the world on her shoulders. Worth nodded her head letting Paisley know I was walking their way. Paisley stood up and walked toward me.

"You need to go find Bull. Someone tried to kill Worth's dad. They made him drink some liquid that caused him to have a heart attack," she said.

"Nah, I'm not leaving y'all here by yourself," I said worried that whoever it was may try to hurt them.

"We're good. Dose got men everywhere in here and outside. I followed Paisley's eyes. I noticed a guy sitting down scrolling through his phone. There was another sitting with a young lady talking. I glanced over the waiting area to see a few more guarding them.

"How's he doing?" I asked glancing at Worth.

"He's going to be okay. He thinks Bull wants him dead. He keeps telling Worth to stay away from him. She's so scared, she made him leave. She's scaring me, Fila. She's talking about aborting her child."

"Don't let her do that dumb shit Paisley. He will fucking kill her," I said. As much as he loves her, it would destroy any love he has for her. I rushed out the door calling Dose.

Basilio

I knew the bitch was going to be mad when she found out I was with Worth. I never thought she would come after her family. Whatever plans I had have changed. I was killing that bitch as soon as I lay eyes on her. She had checked out of the hotel where she was staying. She didn't know New Orleans. There was only one place I knew she could possibly be. I'm sure she knew I was coming for her. I ignored everyone's calls. I know they were going to try and stop me from killing her. No one was changing my mind. If I die, I die. My child will live.

There were guards securing the front and back gates of Sanchez's home. I decided to go to the back entrance. My plan was to be in and out. I waited until one of the guards walked close to me. I was stooped down in some bushes. The other guard was walking in the opposite direction, so his back was facing us. Soon as he got close enough, I jumped and grabbed him from behind. In one quick motion, I snapped his neck. His body went limp in my arms. I pulled him into the bushes. I put the silencer on the gun. I made sure to avoid the security monitors. I had been to Sanchez's house on plenty of occasions. I always scoped out his surveillance. I probably knew his home better than he did. The other guard turned around when I stepped on a stick. He quickly tried to pull out his gun. I had to shoot him before he fired a shot. I let off two rounds. One hit him in the heart while the other one left a hole in his head. His body dropped to the ground. I hurried and pulled him out the way before the camera rotated on his dead body. For the first time, I was thankful he lived in a damn jungle. There were enough bushes and trees to hide behind until I made it to the back door. I smiled when the back door opened. The moment I stepped into the house I heard loud arguing. I recognized her and Moreno's voice. I didn't even know he was in town.

"I told you not to come here. You are fucking up," Moreno said to her.

"That bitch doesn't tell me what to do. I'm supposed to be running this shit anyway. I'm tired of answering to her," Camila stated angrily.

"You don't know him. He will die for his family. He's coming for you. You shouldn't have killed her father," Moreno said.

"You always been a scared little bitch. That's why Daddy left everything to me," she said.

"I never wanted this shit anyway. I got stuck with it. It was either do this or be cut off. I had no fucking choice," Moreno said.

"And you will continue to do as I say or else you will be cut off. Once he dies, we will remove her and control everything. We need him to make that happen. Just for your information I didn't kill the old man. That was that crazy bitch. They fucked up the job. He's not dead."

"Now, we have to take the fucking blame," Moreno ranted.

She laughed. "What can he do? He can't kill us. If he does, he knows his entire family is dead. We are protected by the greatest."

Moreno laughed. "You hate and love her at the same time. You'll never be her. He'll never let you take her spot." I heard a slap. I could only assume she slapped Moreno. I was just about to walk into the room when gunshots started coming from every direction.

"I told you them mothafuckas was crazy!" Moreno yelled. I stayed out of sight until I knew what was going on. I stayed in place until the gunfire stopped. I watched as Moreno ran toward the back door. I shot him in the leg to stop him from running.

"Find that bitch!" I heard Dose order .

"Yo!" I yelled alerting him that I was in the kitchen. "Tell everyone not to kill her." Dose did as I said. Him and Fila walked in the kitchen as I stood over Moreno. He was crying out in pain. I snatched him up by his shirt.

"It wasn't me! I swear I had nothing to do with it!" He pleaded for his life. He could cry blood and I wouldn't give a damn. He was a dead man.

"I want information," I demanded. He looked at me with frightened eyes. "Give me the information or you will die."

"You might as well kill me then," he said. I put the gun to his head ready to pull the trigger.

"Bull, stop it! You can't kill him. If you kill him, you kill all of us. They will seek revenge on the family, not just you," Sheba reminded me walking into the kitchen. By that time Guap walked into the kitchen with a gun to Camila's head.

"You are fighting a losing battle. She'll never let you walk away," she said with a smirk.

"Who the fuck is *she*?" Dose asked looking at me.

"That's what I need to know. First, I want to know why the fuck you brought my sister here," I stated staring at him. I know Sheba could protect herself, but he wasn't supposed to lead her into danger.

"Nigga, she didn't come with us," he stated. He gave Sheba a cold stare.

She shrugged her shoulders. "I followed them. You forget the same man raised me too." She wasn't lying. Sheba would sit for hours and listen to our father tell us things about the business. I thought she lost interest when she fell in love with Dose.

Camila's phone started ringing. Guap had it in his hand. "Let her answer it." I told him. He gave the phone to Camila and she answered.

"Yes," she said before hanging up the phone. We all stared at her.

"She's ready to see you now. She will be here in three days," she said. I couldn't wait to stand face to face with the bitch that has been playing with our lives.

Worth

I hadn't left the hospital all night. I decided to go home to take a shower. He was slowly gaining his strength. I had only left the hospital to shower and eat. I could feel the emptiness in the house when I walked in. He was gone. I could feel it. I knew he wasn't far. There was no way he was walking away that easily . I realized just how dangerous being with him could be. I couldn't live that life. I always felt he could protect me. Now, I'm not sure he can.

Daddy said a woman came to the house with two men. They informed him I was in danger. They told him about Basilio being connected to a drug cartel that wanted me dead. He said he didn't trust them and demanded they leave his house. That's when they forced the glass of water down his throat. He said they threatened our lives if I didn't stay away from Basilio. He said he tried vomiting to pump his stomach, but the drug acted too fast. He felt himself having a heart attack. After taking a shower and scoffing something down to eat, I headed back to the hospital. I was surprised to walk in the room to see Nika sitting there with my parents. Daddy was sleep while Nika and Mommy talked.

"Hi," she said nervously. I spoked before kissing Mommy on her cheek. I walked over and kissed Daddy on his forehead.

"Love just left with her friend. She went to get something to eat," Mommy informed me.

"What friend?" I asked her curiously.

She smiled. "Paisley's brother." I breathed a sigh of relief. I thought he was a good fit for Paisley. He was a respectful young gentleman. She seemed to like him.

"I'm surprised to see you here," I said looking at Nika.

She repositioned herself in the chair. "You know I love their cafeteria food. I came to grab a bite to eat. I saw your mom in the cafeteria. I had to come see him. He was always so nice to me." I remembered how often she would drag me here to eat lunch. I always thought it was weird as hell going on a lunch date at the hospital cafeteria.

"Thank you," I told her. "I was going to call you. I talked to Lamar last night. He said it was okay."

"That's not why I came here, Worth. I truly wanted to see your father."

"I know, Nika. I just wanted you to know about the party. I hope to see you there." Lamar doesn't think she will show up. He said she has canceled on Baby Gladys numerous times. I'm hoping she's true to her word this time.

"You will. I promise," she said with a smile.

"We've been having a nice conversation," Mommy said smiling at Nika. I hope she wasn't going to tell me to give our friendship another try. That wasn't going to happen. My only concern was making peace with my heart.

"What about?" I asked glancing at the me.

"Just girl talk," Mommy said winking at Nika. Nika smiled at her. Whatever the talk was about I hope it helped Nika find the value in herself. I couldn't comment on Nika's life. My life was too fucked up. I was in love and pregnant from a man who's occupation was endangering my family's life. I can't believe I was seriously considering having an abortion. After Nika left, I sat with my parents for about an hour. I had asked Paisley to go to the consultation appointment with me. When I arrived at the clinic, she was waiting in her car. We both got out our cars at the same time. She walked over to me with a concerned look on her face.

"Paisley, I'm not asking your opinion. I just need you here for support," I told her.

"Are you really considering killing your child. This will kill him, Worth. I know you don't want to do this."

"I haven't made up my mind what I'm going to do. All I know is I have to protect my family. Whoever those people are, they don't want him with me. This is the only way I can be sure he will stay away from me."

"He could also start hating you for doing this," she warned me.

"I will make that sacrifice if it's going to assure my family's safety," I said. As we entered the building I could feel eyes watching us. I didn't know if they were guards or the people that harmed my daddy."

"You know they are going to report to him your whereabouts," Paisley warned me.

I knew they were. I was hoping they would. I'm hoping he will be so angry he will walk away from me. This is my body. It's my decision whether to have this baby or not. When I was finally called to the consultation room, I sat and listened to my options. Adoption was not a consideration. I couldn't imagine having a child in this world and not be its mother. After leaving the meeting I wasn't sure what I was going to do. I had already fallen in love with this life growing inside me. Knowing it was a part of Basilio made that love even greater. Paisley didn't pressure me anymore about the pregnancy. Instead we went shopping for Baby Gladys a birthday gift, since we were going to her party in a couple of days. Looking at all the baby stuff made me realize I could never abort my child. My mind wondered how I could have my child and protect my family. It dawned on me as we sat at the food court. We found all kinds of cute outfits for Baby Gladys. We went overboard with toys. I hadn't bought her anything in a long time, so I had some making up to do. Regardless of me and Nika's friendship, she will always be my Goddaughter.

"I know what I can do," I told Paisley as we sat eating. Paisley looked at me waiting for me to speak. "I can leave the country for a while. You know I've always wanted to visit Africa. How fucking awesome would that be to have my baby in Africa?"

"Honestly, it's not a bad idea. You are forgetting one thing. You didn't create that life by yourself. It's his child too, Worth."

The excitement of my idea left as quickly as it came. "I know that Paisley. I want nothing more than to have a life with him and our child. I just don't see how that is possible. Someone came into my parents' home to kill my father because of the man I love. It's like choosing my family or my love for him. I couldn't stop the tears from falling, thinking how hard it is knowing I can't have the love I have fought so hard for. I thought after Majesty, we could be together. Now, we are still fighting for a life together. I'm starting to think I wasn't meant to have a love like ours.

Paisley

After spending the day with Worth, I headed to my apartment. With everything that happened with Worth's dad, I completely forgot to tell Fila about Estelle's blackmail threat. The only way I was giving him up is if he tells me I have no choice. It would break my heart if I had to let him go. I was growing impatient waiting on him. Lately, he's been really secretive about his movements. I played NBA 2K18 until I got sleepy. I took a long hot shower and climbed in the bed. I fell asleep the moment my head hit the pillow.

I jumped out of my sleep when I felt something between my thighs. "Oh, hell no!" I said sitting up in the bed pushing his head from between my thighs.

"What the fuck wrong with you?" He asked staring at me like I was crazy. I jumped out the bed.

"Nigga, this ain't a motel. You don't come here anytime of night. You can take yo ass home. I'm not going to start that kind of shit," I ranted. I snatched my phone off the nightstand and looked at the time. My eyes grew big. "Nigga, it's four o' got damn clock in the morning. You must be out yo rabbit ass mind."

"Calm yo ass down. I was handling business," he said getting off the bed.

"I'm not stupid! Only thing you handling this time of night is a piece of dry ass pussy. You can take yo ass back there. You ain't getting shit here. So, take yo ass home."

He walked up to me and tried to grab me by the arm. "Don't fucking touch me! I don't know where your hands been nigga."

A scowl spread over his face. Before I knew it, he had yoked my lil ass up in the air by my arms and slammed me on the bed. "Damn, I love when yo lil ass get heated. My dick 'about to damn break it's so hard." He whispered in my ear laying on top of me. His wet tongue started licking on my neck. I hated that I was getting moist between the thighs.

"Get off of me, Fila," I said trying to convince myself I wanted him to stop. I was shocked when he actually stopped.

He stared down at me with a stern face. "Every got damn move I'm making is for us. I'm not out there on no bullshit Paisley. I got what the fuck I want with you. If you can't trust me enough to believe that, we need to dead this shit now." I could see the seriousness in his eyes.

I turned my head to keep from looking into his eyes. "Nah, look at me," he said turning my head to face him. "Why the fuck you tripping?"

I closed my eyes. "I'm scared," I said in a low voice.

"Open your eyes Paisley." I slowly opened them. He stared into them.

"I'm not going to hurt you. I'm not going to walk away from you. I got you. You gotta fucking believe that for this shit to work," he pleaded with me.

There was so much sincerity in his eyes. I had to let go of the fear of being broken like my mother. If I didn't, I was going to lose him. I relaxed under him. I slowly spread my legs inviting him between them. He leaned down and covered my mouth with his. He slid his minty wet tongue inside my mouth as his hands pulled down my panties. I assisted him by pulling my shirt over my head. He licked his way down to my breasts . He flicked his tongue over my hard nipples as his fingers played in the puddle between my lower lips. I arched my back letting out a soft moan when his fingers slid inside me. Biting and sucking my breasts while poking my g-spot had me on the verge of exploding. He pressed his thumb against my throbbing clit making circles. I couldn't hold it any longer.

A Love Worth the Fight 3   Nona Day

"Sssssssshhhhhh!! Yyyyeeeeeessss!" I moaned as my body shivered. He pulled his fingers out of me and dove in between my thighs with his face. My body wouldn't stop shaking as he slurped and sucked my creamy fluids. He raised my legs pushing them up to my chest. His wet tongue stroked from my pussy to my ass.

"Oooooohhhhh," I moaned as his tongue played with my ass. He French kissed between my drench lips. His tongue was like a windmill slurping up my juices. He groaned as he gulped down my wetness. "Shit Fila! I'm bout to come again!" I warned him when he started fondling my swollen clit with his tongue. He grunted as he licked and sucked until my essence was gushing over his face.

I lay there unable to move as he kissed his way up my body. I could barely keep my eyes open as I stared at my essence dripping from his beard. I pulled his face to me sucking his bottom lip into my mouth. I had to taste myself on his lips. After ending our kiss, I instructed him to lay back on the bed. He laid back propping his head up on a couple of pillows . I know he wanted a view of me riding him. I straddled his lap backwards. My mouth watered staring at his thick long dick. I had to taste it. I moved backward allowing myself enough space to lean forward. I lapped my tongue around his thick dome. His dick jumped as he moaned. I slowly started sliding him inside my mouth. My saliva was spilling out my mouth soaking his shaft.

"Shit!" He roared as the head of his dick hit the back of my throat. I held it there and reached down to massage his balls with my hand. "Fuck!" He barked. "I'm bout to fucking bust! Ride this dick for me baby!" I did as he instructed. I rode him like a professional bull rider. I bounced and twerked my ass up and down his thick hard pole, until I was screaming and coming at the same time. I didn't stop until I saw his toes cramping.

"Got damn! Aaaarrrrgggghhhh!" I bellowed as he erupted inside me. His body jerked and shuddered until he was finished releasing. He gently smacked me on the ass. "Damn, you got some good ass pussy." I giggled as I tried to get off of him.

"Nah, I want you to sleep just like that for the night. I'm gone take an hour nap and wake back up in it," he said holding me by the waist.

I laughed and tapped his arm. "We gotta talk."

"Damn, you still tripping?" He asked letting me go. I turned around to face him. He was perfect in every way. Just staring at him caused a thumping down below.

"Nah, it's about Estelle," I told him. His entire body tensed up and a frown appeared on his face. His semi hard dick completely softened. I took a deep breath and told him what happened when she visited my apartment. I thought he was going to get furious. He just shook his head.

"Let me handle Estelle. I told you I got you," he said winking at me. I smiled. "Now, don't ever bring her name up while I'm trying to dig in yo guts all night." I laughed.

Basilio

After having Moreno's wound bandaged, we took them to a safe house we had purchased since moving to New Orleans. I can't believe Moreno portrayed himself as the leader for years. Now, he was looking like a scared little boy. Camila held a poker face as she sat on the sofa. I thought of ways of getting the information I wanted from her. I knew I couldn't kill her, but torture wasn't out of the equation. I could hear Dose and Sheba arguing in the next room. I left Guap and Tree to watch Moreno and Camila while I calmed down Dose. He was furious because Sheba showed up at the house.

"Hey, y'all too fucking loud," I said walking into the room. Sheba rolled her eyes at Dose. Dose was pacing the floor.

"She's fucking hardheaded . I told her to stay out this shit!" He barked staring at her.

"I've been in the shit from the start. Don't try and cut me out now," she said. Sheba was right. She was a part of our original plan before Sanchez had Eduardo killed. After we threatened Sanchez's family, we knew he would step down. Dose was going to take my spot in running the family. The only way he could do it was if he married Sheba. Soon as Dose took over, we were going to dismantle the family. We knew it wouldn't be easily done. He was willing to stay in the game until it was done. After our plan blew up in our face, Dose asked Sheba to still marry him. She didn't waste any time accepting his offer. They married in Jamaica while on vacation.

"Yeah , that was before you were my fucking wife and carrying my damn child," he said. Sheba stared at him with murder in her eyes.

"You're pregnant?" I asked. She looked at me with guilt. "Why are you looking like that? Aren't you happy?"

"Yes, but I didn't want to mention it while you were dealing with discovering Worth's pregnancy."

I smiled at her. "I'm going to be a father and an uncle. How far along are you?"

"Three and a half months," Dose answered for her. He stood like a proud father. Besides Worth being pregnant, this was the best news I could've heard.

"That's why I've been gaining so much damn weight. I know you've noticed," she said rolling her eyes at me.

Me and Dose laughed. "All I see is my beautiful baby sister when I look at you."

"All I see is my fat mama," Dose said winking at her. She stuck her middle finger in the air at him.

"Congratulations brother," I said giving Dose a handshake . He nodded his head with a big smile.

"Sheba, stay out this shit. We know you can handle your own but it's not just you anymore. I'll kill you if you harm my niece," I told her.

"Nigga, that's my lil man in there," Dose stated. I laughed.

"So, what are we going to do until whoever arrives?" Sheba asked.

"We aren't going to do a damn thing. I've already told you. You are going to continue running the club and we are going to handle everything else," Dose told her. She started pouting. I just shook my head. He's going to catch hell during this pregnancy.

"Who the fuck are we expecting in three days?" Dose asked me.

I shrugged my shoulders. "Your guess is as good as mine." We didn't have a clue who was arriving. As far as we knew, Moreno was leader of the cartel. We've been working years for a mothafucka we didn't know. I couldn't wait for this meeting. As angry as I am about being played for fools for years, I'm hoping it's someone willing to negotiate our freedom and safety.

"How's Worth's father?" Sheba asked.

"He's going to pull through. I want to torture both of their asses," I said.

"Nah, let's not fuck up our chances of negotiating what we want," Dose suggested. He was right. Whoever was in charge thought they were valuable enough to lead the cartel. I nodded my head in agreement.

"You should be with her, Bull," Sheba said. A sharp pain pierced my heart remembering her telling me to leave the hospital.

"She doesn't want to be near me. I'm responsible for her father laying in the hospital."

"She's just scared. Give her some time. I'm going to go check on her," Sheba said. That made me feel better knowing she would be there with Worth.

"I'll talk to you at the house tonight," she said looking at Dose.

"I'll be ready Fat Ma," he said smiling at her. I laughed as she walked out the room. Dose and I walked back into the room where Moreno and Camila were being held. I sat a chair in front of Camila.

"Who's coming to see us?" I asked calmly.

She smiled. "I wouldn't want to ruin the surprise." I knew she wouldn't tell me but I had one other thing I wanted from her. I could wait to find out who the mystery guest was. I felt like there was a wrong done that I needed to correct right now. I reached out and held one of her hands.

"You have pretty hands. You ever wonder what it would feel like to be without them?" She tried holding a straight face, but I could see the fear in her eyes. I chuckled. "Don't worry. I'm not asking for the mystery guest's name."

"W-what do you want?" She asked. I glanced at Moreno. He sat there like a weak man. I was beyond disgusted with him.

"Moreno, you want out this life?" I asked. He shook his head yes. I could tell he thought I was going to help him.

"Too fucking bad. Until I get my freedom, you won't have yours." Dose, Tree and Guap laughed.

"Release Maria out of the fields," I told her.

She smiled. "I thought you were in love with the green-eyed girl." I shrugged my shoulders not giving her any more information than she needed.

"Fine. I could care less about her," she said nonchalantly.

"You will buy her out of this life. She will walk away with her freedom and safety," I said. I wanted to give Maria the chance to find the love she wanted with me. The only thing she was guilty of was loving a man that didn't love her. She didn't deserve to be slaving in a cocoa field for years.

"Fine," she said rolling her eyes. I nodded at Guap. He walked over and gave her the phone. She made the call ordering Maria back to Baton Rouge.

"You will relinquish all the accounts that belonged to her father," I demanded.

She laughed. "That's pennies to me." This wasn't about her. This was about giving Maria a chance at life outside of this corrupt life.

Worth

"**A**re you going to play with that food or eat it?" Mommy asked looking from me to my kitchen table. I convinced her to come home with us after leaving the hospital last night.

"Are you going back to him?" I asked looking up at her. Earlier today, the other woman showed up to see our father. He declined to see her. I know he was just trying to show Mommy some kind of respect.

"Do you want me to?" She asked glancing at me and Love.

"We want you to do what will make you happy. He said he wants to work things out with you," Love told her.

She smiled. "I will always love your father. I'm just not in love with him anymore. I will do whatever I can to make sure he recovers, but I will not be going back to him." I didn't know how to feel about my parents actually ending their marriage. I was hoping Daddy would realize how much he loves her and stop what he was doing. I didn't factor in Mommy wanting to move on with her life.

"I can't believe she had the nerve to show up at the hospital," Love said shaking her head.

"Obviously, she felt comfortable enough in their relationship to come. I'm going to let her take it from here. If she loves him enough, she'll stick around. If not, she'll run for the hills. He's going to need a lot of care."

"She won't last," I said. Mommy smiled.

"Now, what else is bothering you?" She asked.

I shook my head. "Nothing." She gave me a look letting me know she knew I was lying. I just didn't want to talk about it right now. I didn't want to think about Basilio or the fucked up situation I'm in. It was Baby Gladys' birthday. All I wanted was to see her have fun. I'm praying Nika shows up. I didn't have to tell Mommy what was going on. Love blurted it all out without taking a breath. She sat the staring at me making me feel like a small child about to get her ass beat by her mother.

"Is all this true?" She asked. I nodded my head yes. "Do you love him?" She asked still staring at me.

"Of course I do Mommy, but I'm not willing to jeopardize my family's life," I explained.

"Don't let anyone keep you from what will make you happy in this life. You nor Bull can protect this family. God got us," she said winking at me. "Trust him to do as he says he would. I know he will give his life to protect that little life growing inside you."

"I know he would Mommy. That's the problem. I can't let him lose his life for me. I can just choose not to be with him and we all live," I told her.

She smiled. "Something tells me it's not your choice. I don't think he's going to walk away that easily ." She was right. I hadn't heard from him since I made him leave the hospital, but I knew he wasn't gone for good.

I lounged around the house, until it was time to go the party. Just as we were getting ready to leave the house, Sheba was pulling into the parking lot. I opened the front door to let her in. I stared at the numerous guards surrounding the house as Sheba made her way to the door. The next house was at least a mile away from us. I'm sure there were as many in the back of the house as there were in the front. I felt relieved to see so many men guarding the house. Sheba gave me a hug and we walked to the den.

"You wanna drink?" I asked.

"No, I'm good. I just wanted to come check on you and my lil nephew," she said smiling at me.

"We're good. I know why you're here Sheba. I know he told you I made him leave the hospital."

She smiled. "He did. Worth, you won't be able to keep him from his child. Trust me, I understand why you are scared. I'm sorry about what happened to your father. I promise they won't be touched again. He just needs a little time to work this crazy shit out."

"I don't want to think about this right now, Sheba."

She nodded her head. "I won't stress you about it. I came to talk to you about something else." She looked at me with unsure eyes.

My heart started pounding. I hated not being sure of his safety all the time. "What's wrong?"

She smiled. "I'm pregnant." I breathed a sigh of relief.

"Oh my God, Sheba! I'm so happy for you!" I said excited giving her a hug.

"I was worried about telling you. It seems like it wasn't the right time with all that is going on with you and Bull."

"Regardless, I want the best for you and Dose. I know he's ecstatic," I told her.

"I can't stand him right now," she said rolling her eyes. I laughed. I remembered Mommy telling us how she couldn't stand for our father to touch her doing her pregnancy. I answered my phone when it rang. It was Paisley calling to see had I left for the party yet.

"I won't hold you up. I just wanted to come see you," she said smiling.

"You can tell him I'm doing just fine," I said grabbing my bag on the sofa causing some papers to fall out. Sheba reached down to pick them up. She stared at me in disbelief. I looked at the papers to see they were pamphlets from the consultation I had earlier in the week. I looked at her with shameful eyes.

"It's not what you think. I was just so scared Sheba."

"He will not let anything happen to you or your family again. Please, don't consider doing something like this. That would kill him."

"I'm not," I told her.

Paisley

"Ok, I'll be there shortly," I told Ced over the phone. I was on my way to Baby Glady's birthday party. I had to make a detour because Ced had a flat tire. He didn't want to wait for roadside service. I could never be on time for anything. I made a turn in the road and headed in the opposite direction. I pulled up behind him and hopped out the car.

"You don't know how to change a tire, nigga?" I asked walking up to him.

He laughed. "Yeah , but I never did put the spare in the car. That's why I didn't call Pops. I didn't want to hear his mouth."

I shook my head. "Get your stuff. I'm in a hurry." He grabbed his bag out the car. My eyes grew wide open when a bag of weed fell from his back pack. If looks could kill, he would be dead right now.

"What the fuck Ced?" I screamed at him. I immediately reached down and snatched the bag off the ground.

"It's nothing big. I just hustle a little on the side," he tried explaining .

I lost it and started hitting him. "Are you stupid? You are going to fuck up your future! I can't fucking believe you!" I was brought back to my senses when I heard police sirens. I immediately stuffed the bag of weed inside my jeans. My heart was pounding. I would go to jail before I let him jeopardize his chance at a college scholarship.

"Give it to me Paisley," he demanded gritting his teeth.

"Just shut up and let's get this over with," I instructed him. The cop took a few minutes before coming up to the car. I could feel my heartbeat through my entire body. I glanced at Ced to see him calm.

"What seems to be the problem?" The officer asked walking up to us.

"Nothing officer, just horse playing with my brother. He has a flat tire. He didn't want to wait on roadside, so he decided to aggravate me," I said smiling at the officer. I didn't like the way he looked at Ced. I've seen that look in too many officer's eyes.

"I need to see your driver's license," he said eyeing us. Ced reached in his   pocket and pulled out his wallet. He gave the cop his license. He looked at me. "I need yours also."

A Love Worth the Fight 3   Nona Day

"It's in my car" I stated. He told me to go get it. As I was walking back to my car, an unmarked cop car pulled up . I recognized the man that got out the car, but I couldn't remember how I know him. He walked past me and stood next to the officer. I had an awful feeling in the pit of my stomach. I grabbed my license and walked back over to Ced's car.

"Nah, you don't have a reason to search my bag," he told him. I knew then he had more drugs in his bag.

"Why do you need to search his bag?" I asked them.

The cop that was in civilian clothes spoke. "He's acting suspicious. Search the car." He ordered the cop.

"No! We aren't doing anything wrong. This isn't legal!" I ranted.

"If you refuse, we will arrest him," he said. I felt stuck. Either way Ced was going to jail. Tears started filling up my eyes. We argued back and forth which seemed like forever. A sense of ease came over me when I saw Fila's dad pull over. The plain clothes cop immediately grabbed Ced and slammed him against the car. He locked his hands behind his back. Ced was tussling to get free from him. I started yelling for him to let my brother go.

I heard Fila's dad. "What the hell is going on?" The next thing I know shots were fired and his body hit the road. I stood there unable to speak as I watched his blood spill onto the road.

"He has a weapon," the officer said walking over to his body. I looked on the ground to see his cellphone laying beside him.

The plain clothes officer let Ced go. He walked over and stooped down beside his body. He felt to see if he could feel a pulse. He looked up at the officer. "He's dead." I couldn't control the loud ear-piercing scream escaping from me. Ced wrapped his arms around me as I cried.

"Calm down," the officer said. I wanted to kill both of them with my bare hands. "You either go along with our story or you and your brother is going to jail. We have every right to search your cars and bags now. I'm sure I will find what I'm looking for."

"What the fuck are you talking about?" Ced asked the cop. He searched Ced's bag and came up with nothing. His face turned red. He was furious. I tried to remain calm remembering I had a bag of weed on me.

"Finish searching the car, Davis," the ordered the cop.

Natavia Presents

"You need to call an ambulance. You don't know if he can be saved or not," Ced told him. He looked back over his shoulder at Fila's dad."

"He's dead," he said shrugging his shoulders. I hocked and spit in his face. He was a cold and heartless bastard.

"Well, look what we have here," the officer said walking back over holding a bag of weed.

"Mothafucka, that ain't mine," Ced said launching toward him. The officer pointed his weapon at Ced stopping him in his tracks. I almost pissed on myself I was so scared.

"Please, Ced," I pleaded. I just wanted us to get out of this alive. "What do we have to do?" I asked staring at the heartless cop. He smiled and winked at me making my skin crawl. He told us everything he wanted us to say. I convinced Ced to go along with what he said. I just needed to get us out of this situation. After he was done telling us what to say, they finally called in the murder they just committed. All I could think about was how this was going to devastate Fila.

Fila

"What the hell are you doing here?" Stella asked as I entered Estelle's house. I ignored her. Fiji came running from the back room.

"Daddy!" He screamed jumping up in my arms. "Papa hasn't come to get me."

"I know. I've tried calling him. He hasn't answered," I said. I'm sure he was home sleep. When he goes to sleep, it's like walking up the dead.

"You can't be here," Estelle said standing there with her hand on her hip.

"Go get your things, lil man. I need to talk to your mother," I said putting him down.

He stared up at me with fear in his eyes. "You going to fight?" It broke my heart to think he felt that way every time we were around each other.

"Nah, lil man. We are going to come to an understanding about things," I said smiling and winking at him.

"Then I can come live with you again?" He asked excitedly .

"Yeah , that's right," I told him. He ran to the room to retrieve his things.

"Why would you tell him that? I'm not letting him live with you and that black bitch," Estelle said with anger.

"Come in the bedroom. Let me talk to you a minute," I said walking away. When she walked into the bedroom I was sitting on the side of the bed. She rolled her eyes at me. "Come here, I'm not gone fuck with you," I said licking my lips. A small smile spread across her face as she walked over to me.

I ran my hands up the side of her thigh. "I can't lie. A nigga been missing you. That pussy still tight and wet?"

She shoved me. "Stop playing Fila. Everybody know you in love with that black ass Paisley."

"I ain't gone lie. I like her, but a nigga still got it bad for you," I said.

She relaxed. "So, what does that mean?"

"Shit, I'm trying to slide between them thighs later," I said massaging her inner thighs. "I want to do something special for you. I'm gone drop Fiji off with Pops tonight. I'll be back later."

"Fila, you know Ma staying here since you didn't pay her rent. I don't have any money in my accounts," she said rolling her eyes at me.

I chuckled. "Let's get us straight again. Then, we'll fix all that other shit. I'll come scoop you up later."

"Ok," she said smiling.

"I'm ready Daddy," Fiji said barging into the room. I gave Estelle a peck on the check leaving her standing there blushing.

"I know yo ass up to something," Stella said as I walked past her. I smiled and winked my eye at her. Fiji and I headed to my house. Estelle was too happy to argue with me about taking him. I went by Pop's house to see his car wasn't home. I guess he was out with a lady friend as he would call some female he was fucking on the regular.

"Can we go see Paisley?" Fiji asked happily .

"She'll be over later. You act like you more excited about seeing her than spending time with me," I said glancing at him. He smiled. "Well, she's taken. Get your own girlfriend."

He laughed. "She's too old for me Daddy. I need a job before I can get a woman that old." I laughed and shook my head. My heart smiled when I pulled up to see Paisley's car parked in my driveway .

"Paisley's here," I said smiling at Fiji. As soon as I parked, he jumped out the car and rushed inside the house. I grabbed his bag and followed him. It warmed my heart to see her giving him a big hug. After breaking their embrace, her eyes met mine. I knew something was wrong.

"Fiji, go in your room and play the game. Don't come out until I tell you to ," I said never breaking eye contact with her.

"But Daddy I want to play the game with Paisley," he said.

"Do like I said Fiji. I need to talk to Paisley," I said seeing the tears form in her pretty eyes. He stomped toward his room with an attitude. Tears rolled down her cheeks. All I wanted to do was hold her and take whatever pain she was feeling away. I walked over and wrapped her in my arms. She buried her face in my chest and cried like a baby.

"Baby girl, talk to me. What's going on?" I asked holding her tighter. She mumbled against my chest. I broke our embrace to look her in the eyes. Her pretty face was soaked with tears.

"He only stopped to help us and they…" she was startled by the ringing of my doorbell.

"Stay right here," I instructed her. I tried to go answer the door, but she grabbed me by my arm. She stared me in the eyes with so much sorrow I could barely stand to look at her.

"Paisley, what's going on? Who's at the door?" I asked.

"I-it's about your father," she said as she cried. A sickening feeling was in the pit of my stomach. I walked over to the entertainment center and looked at the security monitor. The police officers were standing outside my door.

"Paisley, what about my father?" I asked walking back over to her. She cried shaking her head no. I tried to remain calm, but I was losing my patience. "Damn it Paisley, stop fucking crying and tell me!" I barked at her.

"He's dead!" She blurted out as she buried her face in her hands. I was paralyzed, I couldn't move. She had to be wrong. I just spoke with him this morning. He was excited about spending the day with Fiji. I prayed there was a misunderstanding as I made my way to the door. The moment I opened the door, I knew she was telling the truth. I could see the regret in the black officer's face. Their voices sounded a million miles away. I felt like the life was draining out of me. My father was my role model, best friend and brother. He was the one I came to when anything seemed to be burdening me. He was the one that taught me how to be a man. I had so much more in this life to learn from him. The only thing I remember them saying was I needed to identify his body. I slammed the door in their face while they stood there.

Paisley was sitting on the sofa rocking back and forth. I needed her to pull herself together right now. I needed to find out what happened to my father. "Paisley, I need you right now. I know this is hard, but I need you to pull it together for me." She looked up at me and nodded her head yes.

"I have to go and identify his body. I need you to stay here with Fiji. He doesn't need to see you like this. Can you handle that for me?" I asked calmly.

"But I have to talk to you. You don't understand," she said wiping her tears.

"We'll talk when I get back. Let me handle this first," I told her. I pulled her in my arms and held her until I felt her body relax. I locked the door on my way out.

Basilio

I was sitting in Sheba's den waiting on Dose. We were expected to be at a meeting in a few hours to meet this mystery person. Something keeps telling me I'm not going to like the outcome of this meeting. I made sure Worth and her family had full security. It's been hard staying away from her. Until I know what we are dealing with, I thought it was best to stay away from her. I started scrolling through my phone looking at all the pictures I had taken of her. I smiled to myself thinking about the life we created growing inside her. Sheba walked into the den taking me out my thoughts.

"Maria is here to see you," she said looking at me.

I hadn't spoken to her since she has been returned home. I wanted to make sure she was doing okay. I nodded my head for Sheba to send her in. When she walked in the room, I was happy to see her looking like herself. She looked scared and nervous. "Have a seat," I told her. She sat on the loveseat next to the couch I was sitting on.

"How are you doing?" I asked her with concern.

"Better, thank you for getting me out of there. I felt like I was going to die. I didn't know how I was going to survive living that way," she said with teary eyes.

"You're welcome," I said nodding my head.

"What do I have to do for you getting me out of there? I know you hate me, so you didn't do it out of the kindness of your heart," she said fearfully.

I chuckled. "You owe me nothing Maria. You were used because of your love for me. I've learned the extremes one will go to for the ones they love. You are young, smart and beautiful. There's someone out there that will love you the way you deserve. You have the opportunity to walk away from this life. Take it and enjoy every minute of it."

She rushed over and wrapped her arms around my neck. "Thank you. I'm so sorry for what I did. I didn't know what she was trying to do. I would've never caused you that kind of pain. I would never hurt Sheba."

"I know, all is forgiven," I whispered in her ear. She relaxed in my arms. We sat and talked before she made her departure. She had plans of moving to Los Angeles to start a new life. Sheba walked back into the room.

"I need to talk to you," she said seriously. She sat in the chair and crossed her legs staring me in the eyes. I sat patiently waiting for her to speak.

"I don't know what's going to happen after this meeting. Regardless, Dose and I will continue to live our lives. I know you don't want to bring Worth into this life if we are stuck in it. Bull, you may not have a choice. She's carrying your child. You can't walk away from her."

Everything she was saying was the truth. Things have changed since finding out she's pregnant. Letting her go wasn't an option anymore. Even if I'm stuck in this life, I will have to make it the best for us. I will do everything I can to protect her from what happened to my parents. I can't imagine walking away from her and our child.

"I have no plans of leaving her, Sheba. I'm just giving her some space. I know she's concerned about her family's safety. I'll decide how to move after this meeting," I told her.

She dropped her head and looked up at me. "I wouldn't give her too much space right now. She's scared and not thinking clearly."

"What's going on with her Sheba?"

"She said it's nothing, but I'm concerned. If something else happens, she might be tempted to go through with it."

"Go through with what?" I asked getting impatient.

She cleared her throat. "She had some pamphlets in her bag about abortions." I jumped up from the sofa. I was beyond furious. I can't believe she would even consider killing our child. If she did, we could never have what we're fighting for. I stormed out the den. I was going to make sure she didn't do something that stupid.

"Bull, calm down. You can't go over there acting a fool. She's already dealing with enough. You have to remember she's not used to dealing with shit like this," Sheba said following me to the door.

"Yo, it's time," Dose said coming down the stairs. I took a deep breath to calm myself. I decided to wait and visit her after the meeting.

"Let's go," I said walking out the house.

Dose set the meeting up at one of our safe houses. It was deep in the woods. We had the house surrounded with soldiers. They were also hiding in the woods. I didn't want any surprises. We didn't know who was coming to meet us. I wasn't taking any chances. When we entered the house, Guap and Tree were sitting there with Camila and Moreno. Moreno was still looking like a scared little boy. Camila sat up straight with her legs crossed and a smirk on her face.

"I thought you had a birthday party to attend," Dose said smiling looking at Tree.

Guap laughed. "I don't know why this nigga fronting like he ain't feeling her. I told him to go and play step daddy. We got shit here."

"Man, fuck y'all. I'm where I'm supposed to be,"
Tree stated.

I chuckled. "Go ahead, fam. We got shit locked
down here."

"Nah, I'm good," he declined my offer. I shrugged
my shoulders. I know he was feeling Nika more than he
wanted to admit. We clowned him a lot about her, so he
pretended not to care. If he felt like he could have
something with her, he can't let what we say stop him. Our
opinion is irrelevant in whatever they got going on.

"It's not a choice, it's an order," Dose said staring at
him. He stared at Dose to see was he serious. Dose didn't
crack a smile.

"Man fuck y'all," Tree said before leaving the
house. We looked at each other and burst into laughter.

"I gotta get the hell out of this city. All y'all some
pussy whipped niggas," Guap said laughing.

"You haven't had the right women," Camila said
staring at him seductively.

"Bitch, I'll spread yo lil stick legs and pop you like
a twig," he said with a mean mug on his face. We laughed,
and she rolled her eyes at him. "Bitch been trying to get me
to fuck her for the past two days." Camila was trying to use

what she had to get out of this situation. Guap answered his phone when it rang.

"The car is coming up the driveway," he said after ending the call . We all sat down eager to see who would come through the door.

Worth

I sat in front of Chuck E Cheese calling Paisley's phone. I could never get an answer. I decided to go inside without her. She was forever running late. I thought she would be on time since she called me to see if I was on the way. I was happy to see Nika sitting down holding Baby Gladys. Lamar was sitting next to them. If I didn't know any better, I would think they were the perfect family. I walked over and greeted them both. Baby Gladys reached for me and I took her from Nika's arms. I sat down playing with her until she jumped from my lap. She started playing with the other kids. I noticed Nika's demeanor changed as she stared past me. I looked over my shoulder to see Lamar's girlfriend coming toward us. Nika jumped up when Baby Gladys ran to her.

"Hey everyone," Kristen said smiling at us all. Nika walked over and snatched Baby Gladys out her arms. She turned to face Lamar who was still sitting. "What the fuck is she doing here?" I felt so awkward being in this situation.

"She's here because she's been playing the role you neglected for a while," he told Nika.

"I can leave. I don't want to ruin her birthday," Kristen said looking at Lamar.

"Nah, you just as much a part of her life as we all are. We good," he said ignoring Nika.

Nika sat down holding her daughter. I could tell she was still upset. She held a scowl on her face as she watched Lamar interact with Kristen. I started to feel bad for her when Baby Gladys whined and reached out for Kristen. I guess Nika brought all this on herself. I walked over and sat next to Nika. "It's going to take time Nika. She's learning you all over again."

She looked at me with sadness in her eyes. "She doesn't even know me anymore." She put her daughter down and watched her crawl to Kristen.

"Oh God, now what is he doing here?" Nika said looking at Tree walking toward us.

"You didn't invite him?" I asked.

"Of course not, why would I?" She asked me.

I laughed. "Because he's your boyfriend, and you actually like the ignorant retard." Tree was disrespectful and rude all the time. For some reason, it seemed like he genuinely cared about Nika sometimes.

"Why you sitting here looking like you need to shit?" He asked Nika. I shook my head and laughed.

"Why are you here?" She asked him with an attitude.

A Love Worth the Fight 3   Nona Day

He looked at her like she was crazy. "You said it's your shawty's birthday. I thought I'd slide through and drop a gift off." He followed Nika's eyes as she watched Lamar and Kristen play with Baby Gladys.

He chuckled. "Oh, you mad because yo baby daddy got some new pussy?"

"Hey, show some respect," I said looking up at him. He would never admit it, but I could see he was hurt by the way Nika was treating him.

"Well, you better put this bitch in check before I do," he said looking down at Nika.

"Introduce yourself, while I talk to Nika," I said snatching her up by the arm. "And show some class, Tree," I said before walking off.

"What are you doing?" I asked staring at Nika. "He's trying to show you he cares. If he didn't, he wouldn't be here. You sitting there mean mugging your ex-husband and his girlfriend in front of him."

"I don't want Lamar, I just don't want another bitch playing mama to my daughter," she said.

"Well, step up and be the mother you should be. You know I don't care for Tree at all, but for him to show up here for you and your daughter says something."

She glanced over her shoulder and saw Tree talking with Lamar. They seemed to be getting along well. "I guess I should be playing nice with what's her face?" She asked rolling her eyes.

"Yes, you should Nika."

"Fine," she said before turning and walking away. I shook my head and laughed.

I walked back over and joined everyone. Everyone was having a good time, but I was starting to worry about Paisley. She hadn't showed up to the party or returned any of my numerous calls. I said goodbye to everyone and left the party. I went to Paisley's apartment, but she wasn't there. I was relieved when I saw her car parked at Fila's house. I was going to cuss her ass out for ditching the party for dick. I knocked on the door and waited for her to answer. I was surprised when Fiji opened the door. I thought Fila wasn't allowed to have him at his house unsupervised. Paisley stood behind him with a worried look on her face. I didn't want to alarm Fiji, so I didn't mention it.

"You shouldn't open the door without asking who it is first," I said smiling looking down at his cute face.

He laughed. "I knew it was you. We saw you on the camera."

Natavia Presents

"Oh, I forgot," I said smiling.

"Fiji, go wash up. The pizza should be here in a little bit," Paisley told him. He ran down the hall. "And stop running."

"Look at you on mommy duty," I said smiling at her. She didn't return my smile. "What's wrong?" I asked with concern.

She shook her head with tears in her eyes. I followed her to the den and flopped down on the sofa. I sat with my mouth open as she told me what happened. I held her as she cried. "I feel responsible for what happened, Worth."

"Paisley, don't do that. It's not your fault," I assured her.

"I didn't get a chance to tell him what happened. He's going to nut up when he finds out . He went to identify the body. I haven't heard from him. I'm so worried," she said.

"He's not going to do anything to risk getting locked up. I'm sure he'll remain calm," I told her. I didn't believe what I said. I just wanted to keep her calm. I only hope he remained calm until he left. I know when he finds out the truth, someone was going to die. I decided to stay there with her praying Fila didn't do anything stupid.

Fila

When I arrived at the hospital, I was given directions to the floor I needed to be on. I felt all eyes on me as I stood there waiting to identify my father's body. I prayed it was a case of mistaken identity, but I felt in my heart it wasn't. Something didn't feel right. I hadn't been told how my father died. I was waiting to speak with the coroner. I don't know if I was paranoid or what, but it felt like everyone was whispering about me. A stout white man approached me. I stood up ready to hear what happened.

"Hello, I'm sorry to keep you waiting. I'm Mr. Stanson, the coroner. And you are?" He asked.

"Mr. McCormick, what happened to my father?" I asked not wanting to deal with the formalities.

I became nervous. I immediately noticed he didn't look me in the eyes. "Follow me, and let's talk."

"Nah, I don't need to follow you no got damn where. Just tell me what the fuck happened to him. Where's his body?" I asked angrily. A cop in civilian clothing walked up to us.

"Mr. Cormick, I'm Detective Smith with internal affairs," he said holding his hand out to shake mine. I looked at his hand making no attempt to shake it . He put his hand down.

"What the hell is going on?" I asked staring him in the eyes.

He cleared his throat before speaking. "There was a situation and your father was unfortunately killed by an officer." Everything around me became red . The next thing I remember is being pulled off the officer and handcuffed. I struggled to get out their grasp. I knew I was fighting a losing battle. I wanted to hurt somebody. These grimy mothafuckas killed my old man. I wrestled with them until I couldn't. I breathed heavily trying to catch my breath. I was taken to a small room. It looked just like an interrogation room at a precinct. The only difference was, it was all white and there was no two-way mirror. The detective and another officer came into the room.

"I know this is difficult to hear. I will tell you everything that happened, but I will need for you to remain calm. I'm going to overlook the assault on me under the circumstances," he said taking a seat across from me. The uniformed officer stood in the corner of the room.

"Your father intervened on a traffic stop. He didn't identify himself when exiting his vehicle. The officer noticed something in his hand. To protect everyone at the scene, the officer fired his weapon. Your father was pronounced dead at the scene."

The mothafucka couldn't look me in the eyes. "What was in his hand?" I asked calmly.

"At the time the officer didn't have a clear visual. Later, the object was identified as his cell phone," he said dropping his head.

"He killed my father for holding a cell phone?" I asked staring at him. "I want to see the dash cam."

He dropped his head. "Unfortunately, they weren't working."

"Ugggghhhhh!" I roared jumping up and flipping the table over. I charged toward the detective as anger consumed my body. An excruciating pain shot through my body paralyzing me. I fell to the floor. My body convulsed and trembled. I realized I had been tased .

I don't know how long I laid on the floor. The pain slowly decreased. I was snatched off the floor and sat in the chair. "One more outburst and I'm locking you up," the detective said.

"Where's his body?" I asked.

"We will take you to identify him. I will need for you to remain calm," he said. This mothafucka wants me to stay calm when I look at my father's lifeless body. I nodded my head. They walked me down a long hall. The officer opened the door to let me in. I stood there staring at the white sheet covering his body. I took a deep breath and walked closer to the gurney. The coroner was standing on the opposite side. He looked at me to get my approval to pull the sheet back. I thought I was ready until he did. My knees buckled. I held on to the gurney to keep from falling. I didn't want to cry. Not here, but I couldn't stop the tears from coming. I touched his face. He was already cold. His color was fading. I realized how much I looked like him. My father was a good man. He didn't deserve this. Whoever did this will pay. I turned to face the detective.

"Who killed him?" I asked.

"You will receive a police report once everything is done," he said nonchalantly. I wasn't stressing him about telling me. I knew it wouldn't take much to find out who did it. I wasn't going to make a fuss about a cop killing an unarmed man. I didn't want this in the public eye. I will be the judge and jury. I leaned down and kissed my father's cold third eye. I nodded to the coroner to cover his body. I had to get out of there. It felt like the walls were closing in. My chest was tightening, and my stomach was rumbling. I hurried out the room trying to get out of the hospital.

"Mr. McCormick, I need you to sign some papers," Detective Stanson yelled as I kept walking. I ignored him and kept walking. The cool air felt good hitting my face. I walked to my car trying to calm my nerves. It didn't work. Everything inside my stomach came out. After emptying my stomach, I got in my car leaning my head back on my headrest. I couldn't get his face out of my head. There would be no more evenings with him. We would sit and talk for hours. He would school me on life. I learned so much from him on how to conduct myself in the streets. He loved me like a father, raised me like a man, and schooled me like a mentor. Fiji would never get to experience what I had with him. His grandfather was taken before he could know how great he was. I couldn't hold the deep cry inside me. I bellowed deeply sobbing as I cried sitting in my car until I couldn't cry anymore. I ignored Estelle's call when my phone rang. All I wanted was to get the name of the cop that killed Pops.

Basilio

Camila laughed. "You could never prepare for this," Camila said looking at me. I ignored her as the door opened. A big fat ass man as dark as midnight opened the door. Camila was right. I could never prepare my heart and mind for what I was looking at. There was no way this was possible. I felt light headed. Everything became fuzzy . Guap rushed over and caught me before I hit the floor. I never completely passed out.

"Hello Son," my supposedly dead mother said to me as she walked toward me. I shook my head trying to get the image of her face out of my head. My mind had to be playing tricks on me. "It's really me." She said touching the side of my face with her hand.

She walked away and stood in front of Dose. "My other son. I have missed you both terribly." Dose stood there staring at her like she was a ghost. In our reality, she was a ghost.

"I'm sure this is a shock to both of you. I know I have a lot of explaining to do," she said taking a seat on the sofa. She glanced at Camila. "Never send a girl to do a woman's job. Camila remained quiet. Moreno smirked.

Natavia Presents

I couldn't take my eyes off her. She was still just as beautiful as I remembered her. She was an older version of Sheba. They had the same body frame and all. I needed her to explain how she could still be alive. We buried her on the same day as our father. I don't understand how she could still be alive and not tell us. I couldn't deny how happy I was to see her. My mind was confused, but my heart was overjoyed. So many emotions were going through me at once. Anger was in my heart also. She has been alive this entire time and kept it a secret from us. I took a deep breath and walked over to her.

"What the fuck is going on?" I asked staring down at her.

"Sit my son, we have a lot to discuss," she said as if I was still the little boy that she remembers.

"How are you still alive?" I asked ignoring her request.

Moreno chuckled. "Enough money can make anything possible." She cut her eyes at him and he dropped his head like a scorned child.

"Things happened so quickly that day. I was taken to protect my life. It was best you didn't know to protect yours as well," she explained.

"You've been in hiding for years. You don't seem to be in fear for your life now. You seem to be the got damn boss of shit," I stated angrily.

"I know you are angry, Basilio. You have every right to be. After I recovered from my gunshot wounds, I was told of your father's death. They wanted his power. They were willing to kill of us to make that happen. With him and me out of the way, it was easy to take. You were given a small portion to keep you in the family. Your rightful place is head of the family."

"Who the fuck is they?" Dose asked walking over and standing by me. She cut her eyes at Camila.

"Our father," Camila spoke proudly.

"Your father ordered my father's death?" I asked staring at her. She didn't speak. She didn't have to. Her eyes told the truth. She held a condescending grin on her face. I should've been confused, because Felipe, their father supposedly died on the same day as my father. Standing here looking at my mother lets me know that wasn't the case. He set things up to kill my father. Family wasn't supposed to kill family.

Pow! Pow! I had pulled my gun out and put two holes in Camila's head. "A life for a life." I said staring at mother.

She smirked. It didn't faze her that I had just killed Camila, Felipe's daughter.

"What about this one. Are you going to kill him too?" She asked glancing at Moreno. Moreno looked up at me with pleading eyes. Something didn't feel right. It was like she wanted me to kill them. I had a feeling Moreno was more valuable to me alive than dead. I decided to spare his life.

"Guap, get rid of this bitch's body," I said. He had a guard take her body out of the house. "You've been staying with the man that killed your husband?"

"I didn't have a choice. I have been a prisoner for years," she said with sad eyes. I was looking at Moreno out the corner of my eye. It was obvious he wasn't believing the bullshit she was spitting to me .

"Now you sit here like Griselda Blanco," I said staring at her.

"Don't judge what you don't know. You don't know the horror and sacrifices I endured to get back to my children. I have missed so much of your lives."

"Where the fuck is Felipe?" I asked.

Moreno chuckled. "He faked his own death only to be on his death bed fighting cancer ."

Dose and I looked at each other. He was a weakened man. We can walk away from this shit. If what Moreno said is true. He doesn't have the power to fight us. I laughed. "Karma is a bitch. I want to see him."

"He sent me on his behalf. You have an obligation to take over the family. If there was any chance of you walking away, you just killed her," mother said with sad eyes.

"Fuck that! I'm not taking over shit! I'm done," I barked angrily.

"He will kill all of us. He wasn't trying to kill her father. That was a message. We have to do what he says." The fear in her eyes looked genuine.

"The fool dying. His punk ass son doesn't want the business, and his daughter is dead. What are we doing this for?" Dose asked angrily.

"He has a son. He's nine years old. He wants to leave him with the most powerful drug cartel ever known. You can make that happen," she said.

I laughed. "He expects us to do this shit until his son is grown?" Her eyes answered the question. "You tell that mothafucka to kiss my ass!"

"He will kill her. He's a dying man, but his reach is far," she said staring at me. She was my weakness. I had to do whatever to protect her. I now know my only way out of this is to kill him. Moreno will be the one to help me to do it. As far as my mother, I'm not sold on her victim act. My gut tells me there's more to her story.

"I'm not doing shit until I speak with him," I told her.

"I can't promise anything. He's requesting Camila and Moreno back home. I will do my best to explain Camila's death," she said. I didn't want Moreno going back to Colombia, but I didn't have a choice. The look in his eyes says he didn't want to go.

"You roll into our lives after being dead and leave just like that. You haven't even asked about your daughter," Dose said.

She smiled. "I don't have to ask. I know everything about all of you. Congratulations on the marriage and baby. I'm so happy to have you as a son-in-law. I'm going to spoil my grand-babies with everything their heart's desire." I hadn't told her about Worth's pregnancy, but I'm sure she already knew. I didn't feel the love from the mother I lost years ago. The woman sitting in front of us wasn't the woman we lost. I felt it in my bones.

Natavia Presents

Worth

I couldn't sleep as I lay in bed. So much was going through my mind. I was worried about my dad's health, family's safety, and Paisley. She was so scared to tell Fila about her involvement with his father's death. I offered to stay there with her until he came, but she wanted to tell him alone. I know Fila's not going to let the court handle the dirty cop's fate. He will put him in a body bag himself. I couldn't blame him. I'm not a killer, but I will kill for my family. On top of everything, I didn't know if I had a relationship with Bull anymore. After making him leave the hospital, I hadn't heard from him.

Love was supposed to be keeping me company, but she fell asleep during the movie we were watching. I finally woke her up and sent her to bed. She told me she found out Cedric was selling drugs and she threatened to tell Paisley. He promised her he would stop. I'm hoping this knocked some sense into his head. I went upstairs and forced myself to fall asleep. I awakened in the middle of the night with a full bladder. I rushed to the bathroom before I peed on myself. I had to remember not to drink so much water before going to bed. After washing my hands, I realized I was hungry. This baby was going to put more weight on me than I need. My heart nearly jumped out my chest when I turned on the lamp on the nightstand. Basilio was asleep on the sofa in the sitting area of the bedroom. I could hear his light snoring as I slowly walked toward him. I stared down at his muscular physique. His tattooed body was perfect. I reached down running my hand over his broad chest and rippled abs. He caught me off guard and grabbed my arm. I squealed as he pulled me down on top of him.

"Bella, are you trying to take advantage of a sleeping man?" He asked.

I wrestled to get out his grip. I stood up and stared down at him. "No, I was not." He smiled as he sat up on the sofa.

"I've missed you," he said looking up at me.

"You must not. I haven't heard from you," I said rolling my eyes at him. I know it was my fault he hasn't been around, but I didn't expect he would stay away.

"I was only giving you space. I wasn't leaving," he said smiling at me. He scooted to the edge of the couch. "You smell good."

He lifted my short chemise and started placing kisses on my thighs. I gasped from the sensation of his wet tongue stroking my thighs. He lifted one of my legs placing my feet on the couch. He licked his way up to my throbbing mound. My knees buckled when his tongue slid between my wet pussy lips. I massaged his head as he slurped the juices pouring from me. His tongue danced in between my lower lips as I moaned with pleasure. He licked and slurped, round and round like a tornado until I cried out his name. Sliding two fingers inside my wet tunnel he sucked on my swollen clit. I gripped his head and fucked his face until my cream was dripping from his beard. I don't know how, but I ended up on the soft plush rug on my back. My legs were spread open in the air with his face buried inside my creamy center. He growled like a starved animal as he licked, slurped, and sucked on me.

"Ooooohhhh ssshhhhit! Basilio, I'm bout to come!" I screamed. That was his motivation to send me into an intergalactic atmosphere. He spread my legs further apart and violated my soaked pussy with his tongue. My mouth opened wide, but no sound came out. My eyes rolled to the back of my head as I erupted again. He pushed my legs up placing my knees on each side of my head. My body shivered and jerked as he slid his tongue from my pussy down between my ass cheeks. After my body relaxed, he climbed on top of me. He placed my legs on his shoulder. My pussy welcomed her best friend inside of her gripping him tightly.

"Fuuuccck!" He barked as he slid deeper inside me. He stroked in and out hitting every sensitive spot inside me. I started winding my hips matching every stroke he gave me. I could feel his hard dick throbbing inside me. I squeezed my walls tighter feeling every vein inside his shaft. His groans became louder. He pulled out of me and flipped me over positioning me on all fours . He wasted no time driving his brick hard dick inside me. He wrapped his hand around my neck pulling my back against his chest.

"Mio para siempre *Forever mine*, Bella" he whispered in my ear as he nibbled on my ear. He started pounding harder and faster inside me. Slapping sounds echoed through the room as my ass jiggled . He gripped my neck tighter. Harder, faster, deeper he continued to thrust inside me.

"Ven conmigo *Come with me,* Bella." He drove his throbbing dick deep inside me hitting my soft spot and pressing against it.

"Aaaaaaahhhh, I'm cooommminnggg!" I screamed as my cream squirted from me.

"Goooottt dddaaammmnn! Sssshhhhit!" He roared like a lion as he released inside me. We both collapsed on the soft rug. He rolled on his back and pulled me into his arms. I laid my head on his chest.

"What are we going to do? Why is it so hard for us to have a life together?" I asked.

"I will do whatever is necessary to make that happen. Your family will not be harmed. I just need you to believe in me and us," he said.

"I do," I said hugging him tighter.

"I found out some unbelievable news today," he said playing in my hair. I slowly sat up to hear what he had to say. He closed his eyes. "My mother is alive. I saw her today." I sat there in shock at the news. I didn't know much about his mother, but I knew how much he loved her. I know this had the be great news for him.

"Oh my God, how?" I asked.

He opened his eyes. "Enough money can make anything possible." I didn't see the joy in his eyes that I expected.

"What's wrong? Why don't you look happy?" I asked.

"Something in my bones is telling me she can't be trusted. I need to find out more information before I let her in our lives. If I find out she's not the mother I remember, I will kill her," he said staring at me with those cold, heartless eyes that I hated seeing.

"Let's just leave. We can move to another country," I told him. I just wanted all of this to be over. It was like we were on a never ending roller coaster.

"If it was that simple, I would. I want you to live a free life Bella. Not a life hiding and scared, Bella. They weren't trying to kill your father. They wanted to scare you enough to stay away from me."

I was tired of everyone interfering with our lives. I wasn't going to give them what they wanted. I want this life with him and I'm not running away from it anymore. "It didn't work," I said smiling at him .

Paisley

 It was almost three o'clock in the morning and Fila still hadn't made it home. I was beside myself with worry. He wasn't answering my calls or texts . I knew he was filled with anger. I didn't want him doing anything irrational. One bad choice will cost him everything. Just as I was going to call him again, the doorbell rang. My heart and stomach dropped. I prayed he was okay as I walked to look at the security cameras. I didn't want to see the cops standing at the door. I squinted my eyes to see the woman standing at the door. I had never seen her before. I debated on whether to answer the door or not. I wondered if Estelle had reported Fiji was alone with Fila. I also wondered did she have information on Fila. I decided to answer the door. I opened the door to see a broken-hearted woman with red eyes. I could tell she had been crying.

"May I help you?" I asked staring at her.

"I'm Hazel, Fila's mom," she said looking me up and down. She was beautiful. Fila looked just like his dad but had his mother's skin complexion. She was medium height with a thick body and small waist. She was dressed in a slim fitting, knee length body dress. The heel on her shoes had to be at least five inches. Her hair was cut in a boy cut. Her face was beat to perfection. She looked like she stepped off the cover of an Essence magazine.

"I-I'm sorry, come in," I said nervously as I stepped to the side to let her in.

"Thank you," she said walking in. "Where's Fila? I know he's heart broken. That old fart was his heart."

"He's not here . I've been trying to call him since he left to go identify the body. He's not replying to my calls or texts . I don't want him to do anything to jeopardize losing Fiji," I rambled.

"Calm down Bonbon, I'm sure he's okay," she stated calmly. "You must be Paisley?"

I was shocked she knew me. He often spoke of her, but never told me he told her about me. "Yes," I answered.

She smiled. "I see why he's so in love. You are just the prettiest lil thing." I blushed. Her smile disappeared as quick as it came.

"I can't believe he's gone. I still loved that man with all my heart," she said with tear filled eyes.

I didn't know what to say. I didn't know how much she knew. I don't even know how she knows. I know Fila hadn't called her. I walked over and grabbed a few Kleenex and gave them to her. She wiped the tears from her face. "I couldn't believe it when Freda called me. I prayed she was mistaken. I booked a flight as soon as I knew it was true." I had no idea who Freda was, but I felt relieved she was here.

"I was there," I blurted out. I just needed to tell someone. I felt like I was keeping a secret that could cost Fila his life. He needed to know what happened.

Her eyes grew big. "What?" She asked. I walked over and flopped down on the sofa. She came and sat next to me. I told her everything that happened. Just as I finished telling her the front door opened and Fila came walking in. We both stood up to greet him. He looked shocked when he saw his mother.

"How did you know?" He asked her.

"You know Freda keeps me up to date with everything," she said walking toward him. She pulled him into her arms and held him. I waited for him to cry, but he didn't. He consoled his mother while she cried. After breaking their embrace, he walked over and kissed me on the cheek.

"I've been calling you," I said.

"I needed to clear my head, Paisley," he said flopping down on the couch.

"I will handle all the funeral arrangements," Hazel told him. He simply nodded his head. "You haven't done anything you'll regret have you?" She asked him.

He stared her in the eyes. "Not yet, but that mothafucka good as dead."

His mother glanced at me. "You two need to talk. I'm going to crash in one of the rooms. I can't bear the thought of staying in his house tonight." My heart started pounding. She wanted me to tell him what happened. I was wondering if he was going to blame me for his father's death.

He stared at me. I could see he had been crying. His eyes were red and swollen. I walked over and sat next to him. "I'm so sorry. I know how much he meant to you." I hugged him, and he held me tight. I could hear him sniffling. He let me go wiping the tears he couldn't hold back.

"You okay? What's going on with you?" He asked with concern.

"Fila, this is so hard to do. I feel like this is all my fault. If he hadn't stopped, he would still be alive," I said anxiously.

"Paisley, what's up. You can't be talking in codes," he said.

I started to cry as I remembered his father getting shot. I couldn't close my eyes without seeing that image in my head. "Two cops had me and Ced on the side of the road. He stopped to make sure everything was okay. He had his cellphone in his hand. The cop said he thought it was a gun."

He sat there staring at me. I could tell he was trying to take in everything I just said. He let out a loud grunt. "What were you pulled over for?" I filled him in on everything that happened.

"I'm sorry. I should've just let them search everything. I just didn't want to ruin my brother's future."

"Baby, this isn't about you. This was about me. They were fucking with you and Ced, because of me. He's a dirty cop that's been trying to get in my pockets. I guess he was going to use your brother to make me pay up," he explained.

My eyes grew wide. I finally remembered. "He's the one that came here the other day?" He nodded his head yes.

"I had to pay his grimy ass not to arrest you. Estelle had pressed charges on you for whooping her ass. Now, everything made sense. It still didn't take the guilt I was feeling away .

"First thing I'm going to do is lay my father to rest. Everything and everyone else will be handled accordingly," he said.

"You can't risk killing the cop that killed him," Hazel said walking into the room.

"I'm not going to touch him," Fila said. "I've learned a few things about the mothafucka in the last few hours. I'm going to let Cora handle this."

I didn't know who Cora was. His mother joined us in the living room after realizing she couldn't sleep. I listened as they reminisced about times with Carl. I learned that even though they still loved each other, they outgrew each other. Carl was a simple man that loved his hometown. Hazel wanted the fast city life. She wanted to live a somewhat glamorous life. She wasn't one of those women that wanted everything handed to them. She was ambitious and beautiful. She was a well known stylist that a lot of celebrities used.

"You remember when we asked you who you wanted to stay with?" She asked Fila with a smile.

"Yeah , I said you even though I wanted to stay here with Pops."

"You didn't want to hurt her feelings?" I asked.

"It wasn't that. His daddy always told him a man protects the woman he loves. Since I was the woman he loved , he felt it was his place to go and protect me," Hazel said smiling at Fila.

"As far as I was concerned, you was the only woman I was gone love," Fila said laughing.

"Now, look at you. All in love with Bonbon here," she said smiling at me. I had no idea why she called me that.

"Bonbon?" Fila asked laughing.

"A sweet, little chocolate drop," she said winking at me. "I'm so glad you got rid of that other damn girl. I always told you it was something about her I didn't like."

He laughed. "You didn't like her because her mama tried Pops."

"Damn right, like mama like daughter. I was going to fuck that bitch up that night in the club," Hazel said. I giggled. She told me the story about Estelle's mom trying to have sex with Carl in a club years ago. We sat and talked until the sun was coming up. None of us could sleep, so I helped Hazel cook breakfast. I tried to get Fila to get some sleep, but he left the house as soon as he ate, took a shower and dressed. I only hope he remembered the lessons his father taught him about moving in silence.

Basilio

I awakened with the feeling of her wet, soft lips sliding up and down my shaft. Saliva poured from her mouth as she slurped and sucked . Her soft moans were sending vibrations through my dick causing me to groan out loud. "Sssshhhit!" I bellowed when she dipped down and softly slurped my full balls into her mouth. She massaged them with her tongue as she stroked my rock-hard shaft with her soft hands. I felt the tingling sensations running up my spine. She sucked me back into her mouth going deeper and faster. I felt the head of my dick hitting her throat. My toes curled, and my body jerked as I exploded inside her mouth. She slurped and gulped every drop while she massaged my balls. "Fuuuccckkk!" I roared gripping a handful of her hair. She looked up at me and smiled. She kissed the dome of my soft dick and climbed out of bed.

I watched her as she tried to tame her wild hair. She hated her hair. She complained about how easy it tangled. I loved everything about it. She was perfect in every way to me. The baby weight was only adding more sexiness. I smiled as I looked at the little pudge that held our life inside it. I imagined what it would be like raising our child.

Natavia Presents

I wanted the chance to enjoy life with them without the threats from my life looming over them.

"What are you smiling at?" She asked glancing at me. "I bet it wouldn't be funny if I cut it all off."

I laughed. "It wouldn't matter to me Bella. You still would be beautiful." She smiled as she walked and sat next to me on the bed.

"Will I get to meet her?" She asked. I didn't know if I wanted her near my mother. I wasn't sure if she could be trusted.

"I don't know Bella. There's still so much I don't know. It's hard to believe she's completely innocent in all this. My gut is telling me there's more to it than she's telling us."

"How would you find out?" She asked.

"Moreno is the only one that can tell me the truth. I have to get him alone to talk to him. She took him back to Colombia with her," I told her.

"I know you're going there. I'm going with you. You are not leaving me again," she said staring at me. I had no intentions of leaving her again. Where I go, she goes. I simply nodded my head.

She planned to visit Paisley and I needed to discuss our mother's arrival with Sheba. Love was in the kitchen cooking breakfast when we finally made it downstairs. She was on the phone with tears in her eyes. I prayed no one had harmed their family. After she hung up, she looked at Worth. "What is it now?" Worth asked.

"A cop killed Fila's dad," she said. Worth flopped down in the kitchen chair. She was stressing so much. I worried about her and our child's health at this point. "Paisley and Ced saw everything. He had a cellphone in his hand. The cop said he thought it was a gun," she informed us.

"I have to go see her," Worth said jumping up from the chair.

"Worth, you gotta calm down first. I'm not letting you go anywhere upset. Eat some breakfast, and I'll go with you." I needed to check on Fila anyway. I know he has blood on his mind right now. I needed him to be smart in whatever moves he makes. She ate in a hurry. Fila wasn't there when we arrived. I left her there with Paisley, Fiji and his mom.

I was surprised he answered my call. "You need anything?" I asked.

"Nah, I got this. Don't worry. I'm not making any noise," he said. Whoever the cop was I knew he was a dead man. I just wanted to make sure nothing pointed back to him.

When I walked in Sheba's house, I could hear her mouth. She was raising hell. I walked into the den to see Dose sitting there watching ESPN like she wasn't even in the room. I looked at him like he was the crazy one. He shrugged his shoulders. "I'm used to it."

"Why the hell didn't you call me?" Sheba asked staring at me. "She's my mother too."

"I'm not sure she's the mother we remember. Shit didn't feel right Sheba."

"I don't care. I should've met her too," she stated angrily.

"You ever thought to ask yourself why she didn't ask to see you?" Dose said looking up at her. She looked at him without speaking.

She flopped down in the chair and started crying. Dose and I looked at each other. I shrugged my shoulders. I didn't know how to console her on this one. It was his job to handle this. I know she's confused and hurt. I didn't know how to feel about our mother returning. Dose sat next to her and comforted her.

"Yeah ," I said answering my phone.

"There will be a private plane to pick you up tomorrow," Mom said over the phone. "Bring my daughter. I can't wait to see her." I ended the call without responding.

"We're going to see her tomorrow. She asked you to come. Sheba, I need you to remember what and why we are doing this. Don't let her or anyone get in your head." Sheba was vulnerable right now. She needs to feel her mother's love. I don't want her taking advantage of Sheba's vulnerability.

"Why do you think she wants to hurt us. She's our mother, Bull," she asked.

"Gut feelings don't lie. Dose, tell Guap to take a team on our private plane. We gotta figure out how to get to Moreno."

"We're going to need more than a team if shit goes wrong," Dose said.

"I know. I'm going to cover that. I gotta handle a few things before we leave tomorrow. I'll holla at y'all later," I said before turning to walk out.

"She's going to get tired of you leaving her, Bull," Sheba said stopping me in my tracks.

"I'm not leaving her. She's going with us," I told her. I left to secure her family before we left for Colombia.

Worth

"**G**-Ma, can we go see Papa?" Fiji asked his grandmother as we sat in the restaurant eating lunch. She looked at him with so much sadness in her eyes. Paisley stood up and walked out the room. I guess it was too hard for her to tell Fiji about his Papa.

"Come here baby," Veronica, Fila's mother said to him. He walked over and sat next to her on the sofa. I decided to give them some privacy. I walked into the kitchen where Paisley was sitting at the table with her head down.

"It's not your fault Paisley," I said sitting down across from her.

"If he hadn't stopped, he would still be alive," she said looking up at me. "He stopped to make sure I was okay."

"That doesn't make it your fault. Everything that happens is in God's plans. I don't have the answers for you. Somethings are not meant for us to understand," I said to her.

"He says he doesn't blame me," she said referring to Fila.

"Of course not. You did nothing wrong, they did. So, stop blaming yourself," I told her. She gave me a weak smile and nodded her head.

"I wish I could stay, but they are releasing my dad today. I have to pick him up," I told her.

"Where's your mom?" She asked curiously.

"She's living for her now. She said she will do whatever she can to help him recover, but she will do what makes her happy first. She's working and decided not to take the day off. I can't say I blame her. His mistress hasn't been back to see him since he made her leave that day. I think she saw his condition and realized she didn't sign up for all that."

Paisley shook her head. "That's sad.'

"Nah, that's karma. I hate this happened to him. I'm going to be there to help him through this. I feel somewhat responsible. I'm going to move him in with me until he is well enough to take care of himself."

"How does he feel about that?" She asked.

"He doesn't like it, but he doesn't have a choice. He's the reason his wife isn't home to take care of him," I said. She nodded her head in agreement. We sat and chatted about her brother. He promised her he was done selling drugs. She discovered he was pushing drugs to rich white kids.

Veronica walked into the kitchen and sat at the table. "Where's Fiji?" Paisley asked.

"He cried his lil heart to sleep. I know this hard for you Bonbon, but I'm going to need you to grow some tough skin. I can't leave my two men in the care of a weak woman."

"I'm not weak," Paisley stated with an attitude.

"You should've sat there with me while I told him about his grandfather. You plan to be in his life, you need to know how to handle the sad times as well as the happy times. It's not always going to be roses being a stepmother," she told Paisley. Paisley's eyes grew big as well as mine. I guess we never truly thought about her situation. Paisley will be a mother figure in Fiji's life.

"You're right. I'm sorry," she said.

"That's okay Bonbon. You still learning. He will have questions. Answer them the best you can. If you don't know how just call me." Paisley smiled.

I stayed until it was time to pick up my father. He debated with me the entire ride to my house. I was surprised to see a car parked in the driveway when we arrived. I didn't have to wait long to see who was at my house. The front door opened. A tall white guy dressed in scrubs came out. I had no idea who he was and why he was here.

"Hi Ms. Plenty, my name is Carlos. I'll be your Father's Day time orderly. The nurse will arrive in about an hour," he said with a smile.

I looked at him like he was crazy. "Excuse me?" I looked over his shoulder to see Bull standing in the doorway . I walked past the guy. "What's going on?"

"He needs round the clock help. I have a nurse and an orderly that will be here day and night," he said. "You have our life to tend to. I don't want you stressing." I have to admit I had no idea how I was going to care for my daddy. All I know is I had to do it. Knowing I had help was a burden off my shoulders . I know Love will do whatever she could to help, but I know it still would be a lot for both of us.

"Thank you," I said smiling at him.

He winked at me. "You want to take a trip with me?" He asked. I glanced over my shoulder watching the orderly get my daddy out the car.

"I can't just leave him," I said.

"He has around the clock care, Worth. There's a chef that will cook three meals a day for him. A housekeeper will make sure the house is clean," he informed me.

"Where are we going?" I asked.

"I promised you I wouldn't leave you again and I'm not. I have to go to Colombia. I'm taking you with me. This is my chance to walk away from this life. Will you go with me?"

A big smile spread across my face. I would go anywhere with this man. "I have to make sure it's okay with my father and Love."

"I'm cool with it," Love said popping up behind Bull with a bowl of ice cream. I smiled at her. "I'll be here to entertain pimp daddy," she said referring to daddy. I giggled.

The orderly put Daddy in his bed. I climbed in the bed and sat next to him. "She's not coming back is she?" He asked about Mommy.

"She'll be around to help care for you . Right now, she wants to enjoy life for herself," I answered. He simply nodded his head.

I was shocked when he told me he asked his girlfriend to pick him up. She told him she wasn't able to care for him and ended things. He seemed more angry than hurt. I guess he sees the mistake he made. He apologized repeatedly for what he did. My only complaint was if he hadn't had the heart attack, he would still be having an affair. He eventually fell asleep on me. When the nurse came into the room, I left out. Basilio was in the bedroom packing.

"What kind of clothes do I take?" I asked flopping down on edge of the bed. "When are we leaving? How long are we going to be gone? Is this a dangerous trip?" I had so many questions.

I chuckled. "It's hot there. Unfortunately, this isn't a vacation. You can dress casually. I don't plan for us to be there long. You won't be in any danger Bella."

"What about you? Will you be in danger?" I asked.

"No, I'll be fine. Dose and Sheba are going with us. Our mother wants to see her."

"Will I meet her?" I asked. I wanted to meet the woman that created such an extraordinary man.

"We will see Bella. I want to handle business first."

Fila

"**W**here the fuck is my son? He better not be with that bitch!" Estelle yelled as I walked into the house. I ignored her and walked to Fiji's room. I started packing his game systems and clothes.

"What the fuck are you doing?" She screamed trying to stop me.

"I'm calling the police!" Stella yelled barging in the room. I dropped the clothes in my hand and turned to face her. She saw the anger in my eyes and backed away. I walked toward her backing her against the wall.

"You won't call shit. If you do, I may go to jail, but I promise you will be dead. My son will be living with me from this point on. Estelle will drop the custody battle. If she doesn't, your son is dead. Your grimy ass daughter brought the law into my life. She is the reason my father is dead." I turned to face Estelle. "Don't fucking try me. I will kill you." They both stood there with wide eyes full of fear. I finished packing Fiji's belongings. I spun around to face them before walking out the room.

"I want you out of this house by the end of the month."

Natavia Presents

"You can't do that! This is my home! You can't take my home and my son!"

"Watch me," I said before turning and walking away.

"Fila, I wasn't working with any cops. I'm sorry! I never meant anything to happen to your father!" She screamed as she followed me outside. I ignored her and kept walking.

"Nigga, I have evidence that will put you away for life. You better think twice about what you are doing," she said as I opened the car door.

I turned around and chuckled. "Threaten me again and see how many more breaths you take."

"Set that shit up," I said over the phone as I drove home. I was done playing the nice guy with Estelle. She caused enough havoc in my life. It was time to bring it all to an end.

When I arrived home, Ma told me she told Fiji about his grandfather. I went to his room and had a long talk with him. His little heart was broken. "Daddy, I'm going to miss Papa. We have so much fun together."

"I know lil man. I'm going to miss him too. We'll still do fun things together," I said forcing a smile.

"How did he die?" He asked. This was hard to answer. How do I tell my son the men that are supposed to protect and serve us killed him? I didn't want him to grow up being afraid of the police. I didn't want the anger in my heart to seep into his. He was too young to feel those emotions.

"He was accidentally shot" I replied.

"Is the bad man in jail?" He asked.

I pondered on how to answer the question. "Not yet, but he will pay for taking your grandfather from us, I promise."

He nodded his head. "Daddy, you got all my stuff. I can live with you now?" His little eyes lit up looking at all his belongings.

"Yeah , you live with me now," I said smiling. He smiled and wrapped his little arms around my neck. I promised myself I would raise him to be the man my father wanted him to be.

"Daddy, can Paisley live with us too? She plays the games better than you," he asked.

I laughed. "I'll ask her and see what she says." He smiled.

Paisley was sitting on the edge of the bed when I walked into the bedroom. She looked nervous. I walked over and sat beside her. She stared at me with worried eyes. "I don't want you to go to jail. If you kill him, they will lock you up forever."

"All I wanna do is kill the mothafucka. I'm not going to do it though. I can hear my father's words in my head telling me to think before I react."

She looked at me with soft eyes. "Your mother rightfully scolded me today. I couldn't stand watching her tell Fiji about your dad. I realized if I'm going to be with you I'll be more than just a friend to him. I don't know if he understands what that means. He may not be willing to accept me as a motherly figure in his life. I don't want him to feel like I'm trying to take his mother's place."

I lifted her up and sat her in my lap. "I don't expect you to take her place. Estelle was a good mother until her secrets came out. I know you didn't sign up for this. If being his stepmother is too much, I understand."

Her eyes grew wide. "No, it's not. I just know I have a lot to learn. I don't know how to handle the hard times with him. I gotta learn how to chastise and discipline him. I want to be with you and him."

I smiled at her. "I'll be there to help you with everything. You won't be doing this alone. We'll sit down and talk to him about our relationship and family."

She smiled and stood up. "Now, I have to wash some clothes. You have clothes for weeks piled in the laundry room. Got yo mama thinking I'm a pig."

I laughed as she walked out the room. I called Bull to let him know I needed a shipment. "I'll get it done. I'm leaving town in the morning. I'm not sure when I'll return. I'll hit you up when it's due to arrive."

"Good lookin', I'll have Tree pick it up when it's time," I told him.

I went downstairs to the laundry room. "You forgot some clothes," I told Paisley.

She propped her hand on her hip. "Why didn't you bring them down here?"

I pulled my shirt over my head. "You wearing them," I said sitting her on the washing machine.

She giggled as I started removing her clothes. I cupped her breasts with my hands. My tongue lapped around her dark circles. I softly bit her hard nipples as my fingers explored the wetness between her lower lips. Her walls gripped my fingers as I slid two inside her drenched tunnel. She unfastened my jeans as I licked and sucked her breasts. I looked up at her when I felt the washing machine start going. She smiled at me before sucking on my bottom lip. I was ready to slide inside her, but she stopped me. She gently pushed me back. She leaned back and slid her finger inside her wet pussy. She massaged her clit as I watched with an aching and throbbing dick. She stared at me as she continued to bring herself to an orgasm. Her body vibrated along with the washing machine. She bit on her bottom lip as moans of pleasure escaped her mouth.

"That's it baby, make that pussy come for me," I said as my mouth started to water. I could smell her sweet pussy scent in the air.

"Aaaaaahhhhh!" She moaned as her cream spilled from her onto the washer. She placed her cream covered hand to my mouth. I licked and sucked her fingers clean. I wrapped her legs around my waist and slid my dick inside her tight creamy pussy. I couldn't stop the groan from feeling her tight walls gripping my dick.

"Damn, this pussy feels good," I moaned as I slid in and out of her. I lifted her legs placing them on my shoulder. I started driving harder and faster inside her. She cried out in ecstasy as I drilled deeper and deeper.

Oooooohhh! Don't stop!" She screamed as I repeatedly hit her g-spot. Sweat dripped from our bodies as we continued bringing each other to satisfaction.

"Shiiiittt!" I barked feeling myself getting ready to explode. Tingling feelings ran down my spine as my toes started to curl up. "Come on this dick, baby." She threw her head back as her body stiffened and trembled. I rammed inside her.

"Aaaarrrrggghhh!" I bellowed erupting inside her.

Bang! Bang! Bang! She jumped from the banging on the laundry room door. "Shut up all that shit down there!" Ma yelled. I laughed as Paisley covered her face with her hands from embarrassment.

Basilio

The only people on the private plane were the pilot, me, Worth, Sheba and Dose. Worth slept with her head on my shoulder. I started second guessing myself about bringing her with me. None of us knew what we were walking into. I didn't like the thought of risking her life. I hated the thought of her doubting I would return even more. I made sure that she would have the protection she needed if things got crazy.

"Y'all couldn't wait until we landed?" I asked staring at Dose and Sheba as they sat down. They had been in the private room for too long. Dose shrugged his shoulders and smiled.

"I spoke with Orpheus. Everything is in place. We will be the distraction while they take Moreno. We need to get whatever information we can from him as quick as possible."

"You stay back and question him. I'll take Sheba with me. We'll be able to keep our mother occupied for a while."

"Why are you speaking of her as if she is against us?" Sheba asked.

"You didn't meet the woman we met the other day. She wasn't the loving, caring person we remember. She seemed heartless and unsympathetic. I may be wrong. I'm not taking any chances. As far as I'm concerned, everyone is the enemy until I prove otherwise."

Worth slept until we landed. I know she was exhausted. She hasn't had the chance to relax and enjoy being pregnant. A stretch limo was waiting for us when we walked off the plane. We slid inside the limo and headed toward an unknown location. We had plans of getting hotel suites, but she insisted we come straight to the house. I suspected she didn't trust us no more than we trusted her. We finally arrived to our destination after riding for over an hour. The landscape was like a hidden Garden of Eden. The landscaping was designed with beautiful wild flowers, trees and shrubs. Tall palm trees aligned both sides of the long driveway.

The mansion was enormous and sat on a hill. The east and west wing sat just as tall as the main entrance. It was made of white brick with Palladian windows. There was an underground garage that held over ten cars. We pulled into the garage and I counted six limousines. We entered the house through the garage entrance. The white walls were decorated with expensive antique paintings.

Antique furniture and sculptures decorated every room we walked through. We eventually made it to a room which I assumed was the den. There were so many rooms in the mansion I couldn't decipher one from the other.

"Mrs. Vega will be with you shortly," the butler said before exiting the room. Worth and Sheba looked nervous. Me and Dose sat quietly. We're pretty sure we were being recorded. We remained quiet until she arrived.

"Sorry to keep you waiting," she said. She was dressed like the eloquent, classy woman she was. She wore a white, two-piece suit with nude colored high heeled shoes. We all remained seated.

"Oh my God! Look at you. You are absolutely beautiful," she said looking at Sheba. Sheba stood up nervously. Our mother walked over and pulled her into her arms. I could hear soft sobs coming from Sheba.

"I can't believe it's you," Sheba said after breaking their embrace.

"I know it's hard to believe. I'm so sorry I had to stay away for so long," Mother said with tears in her eyes. "I can't wait to be a grandmother. Congratulations on your wedding and the baby."

"Thank you. Dose and I are very happy," Sheba said glancing over her shoulder at him. The look our mother gave Dose didn't go unnoticed by me. It was obvious she didn't approve of their relationship. She gave Sheba a half smile.

"And you must be Worth?" She said walking over to Worth.

"I'm sure you know who I am, since you tried to kill my father," Worth said surprising me. She stood up to face her. My mother was much taller than her. Worth looked up staring her in the eyes.

Mother smiled at her. "If I wanted him dead, he would be dead Sweetie. I don't want to be your enemy. You are carrying my grandchild. I want us to be the best of friends."

"Well, make a way for your children to walk away from this life. They deserve better," Worth said. I was shocked at how she confronted my mother. I thought she would be intimidated by the woman that birthed me.

"I want nothing but the best for my children. I will kill anyone that steps in the way to make that happen," she said staring Worth down.

I stood up and stepped in front of Worth. I knew that was a threat to Worth. "You don't want to do that," I said staring Mother in the eyes. Her eyes softened. "Where is the old man?"

"He only wants to speak with you," she said glancing around the room. That was exactly the way I wanted it. "I've had dinner prepared for everyone in the dining hall."

"I will accompany you," she said glancing at me. I simply nodded my head.

Worth stared at me with wary concerned eyes. "It'll be okay. Just stay with Sheba and Dose until I return."

"Actually, I would like for Dose to meet with the soldiers that he will lead," she said smiling at him. She was smart. She wanted to keep eyes on him. Dose smirked and simply nodded his head. Sheba stared at me. She felt what I tried explaining to her about our mother.

"Come," she said looking at me.

I followed her down a long hall that seemed to never end. We stopped in front of two tall double doors. The room looked as though I was in a hospital. There were machines by the bed. I could barely see the man hooked to all the equipment. I walked closer to him. He was a frail, skinny man. He started coughing uncontrollably. A nurse that I never noticed in the room came rushing to his side. She held a napkin to his mouth until he stopped. The napkin was splattered with blood when she removed it.

"You look just like your father," he said through shallow breathing. He coughed a little more.

"What do you want from me and my family?" I asked.

He called the nurse over with a hand signal. She came over and positioned his hospital bed to where he was sitting up. "I need you to save my family like I saved your mother. I wanted to kill her and your father. I had her removed from the hospital and pronounced dead."

"Why did you save her?" I asked glancing at Mother.

"I felt she was more valuable alive than dead. Your father refused to fight the Ortega Cartel when they came for me. Your mother used her alliances to pull a stronger army together. I was able to keep them from taking over our territory. I owe her everything."

"The Ortega Cartel has raged war on every cartel in Colombia and Mexico. My army is weakening. Your mother's weight doesn't hold as much power as it once did. No one fears her anymore. I know your father's blood runs deep in you. You know how to fight battles. I need the strength of your father behind me to destroy them. You carry that strength. I've worked too hard to let someone take everything I've built for my children."

"I killed your daughter. If I do this, I would have to be in complete control of this cartel until your son comes of age," I said.

"That is true, but you will be the most powerful man in Mexico and Colombia. I have many politicians in my pocket. They will be at your disposal for whatever you want."

"I don't want the power or the money. I have enough money to last me a lifetime. All I want is my family's freedom."

"You will have that eventually," Mother said joining the conversation.

"What do you get out of this?" I asked staring at her. I know there has to be something in this for her.

"I get to walk away and enjoy a life with my children and grandkids," she said.

"And if I don't do this?" I asked looking at Manuel Moreno. I remembered him when I was a young boy. I was blessed with his presence only once. His presence alone showed strength, courage and fearlessness. Now, he looked like a man barely able to fight for his own life.

"Your family will be destroyed," he said. Even though he was a dying man, I didn't take his threat lightly. I know his power reached far . He could be dead in his grave and still bring harm to my family.

"I could kill you now and end all of this," I tried calling his bluff.

"If you believed that, you wouldn't be here," he said. He was right. "Louisa will discuss further plans with you."

I glanced at my mother. I could tell she was more than satisfied with this meeting. She knew I couldn't walk away from what I had to do. Mother escorted me out the room. I followed her down another long hall. We entered what I assumed was a study. It looked like a library. The tall walls were stacked with books. She sat behind the tall, executive desk.

"We are not going to wait for them to come to us. We are taking the war to them," she stated. I sat and listened as she laid out a plan that was never going to happen. I had no plans of going to war with the Ortega family.

Worth

"That's not our mother. I don't know who that woman is," Sheba said with sad eyes as we sat in the dining hall. Food was laid out on the table like a feast. I had no appetite.

"What's taking them so long to get back?" I asked concerned about Basilio and Dose. Dose walked into the room just as I asked the question. Sheba ran to him and wrapped her arms around him.

"I need a distraction. Moreno is in the house," he said after breaking their embrace. He glanced back over his shoulder at the two guards standing at the door.

"They'll never let you out of their sight," Sheba said in a low voice.

"I'm not the one going to get him. I just need you to pretend you are in pain."

Sheba walked over to the table and sat down. She started eating some of the food. I had no idea what she was doing. Dose sat and watched her. About thirty minutes later, he nodded his head at her. She walked over to the guards at the door.

"It's something wrong with my baby. You have to get me to a doctor," she said bent over in pain. They both looked at each other.

"Don't just fucking stand there, get a fucking doctor!" Sheba fell to the floor in pain. They both scurried away for help.

"Stay here with her. I won't be gone long," Dose said before rushing out the room.

Sheba remained on the floor until a stout white woman appeared. "I'm not a doctor, but I'm a nurse. What kind of pains are you having?"

"She's pregnant. I think it's her baby. She could be having a miscarriage," I lied. She wailed out in pain to keep them distracted.

"Oh my God! Get her up to a room immediately. I'll call the doctor," the nurse said hurrying off.

A few minutes later, Basilio came rushing to Sheba's side with his mother. He kneeled down beside her. She had to pretend to still be in pain, because their mother was looking over Basilio's shoulder. "Get her upstairs now!" She barked at the guards.

"Nigga you touch my sister, you dead," Basilio said lifting Sheba in his arms.

I followed behind them as they followed the guards to a bedroom. He laid her in the bed. He still didn't know she was faking. "What happened?" He asked looking at me.

I shrugged my shoulders. "I don't know. She ate some food, then got sick." I couldn't tell him the truth, because the guards were still in the room.

"Oooohh, it hurts so bad," Sheba cried out balled into a fetal position.

"Fuck this! I'm taking you to the ER!" Basilio said rushing over to the bed.

"We will see if the doctor is on the way. The hospital is too far away. Mr. Moreno's doctor doesn't stay far from here," one of the guards said. He looked nervous and scared. They rushed out the room.

Basilio sat on side of the bed with Sheba. "I'm not hurt. Dose needed a distraction. He said he'd only be gone for a short time. He's been gone too long," She whispered to him.

"I'm getting you and Worth the fuck out of here. Shits about to go bad in here," he said standing up.

"I will get us out, I promise. I need you to go find Dose," Sheba said. He looked at her as if she was crazy. "Please, Bull. I promise. I will protect her with my life."

He walked over and stared into my eyes. "Te amo *I love you*, Bella." He leaned down and covered my mouth with his giving me a deep kiss. I wanted desperately to tell him to leave with us. I knew I couldn't. I couldn't ask him to leave Dose here to fight this battle without him. The two guards ran into the room. They were met with bullets to the dome. Basilio shot them so fast I never heard the shots go off. I looked at the gun realizing he had on a silencer. Sheba ran over and grabbed their guns.

"Don't forget everything you have learned. Father taught us well," Basilio said staring at Sheba. She nodded her head. Basilio checked the hallway and gave us the okay to leave the room. We hurried out in a different direction.

"Where are we going?" I asked.

"To the garage. We have to get to the cars," Sheba said as we rushed down the halls. We were met by another guard. He wasted no time firing shots at us. She pulled me behind a tall statue. My heart was beating a mile a minute. I saw no way that we could make it out alive. There were entirely too many guards on the premises.

Pow! Pow! I peeped over Sheba's shoulder to see the guard's body on the floor. Guap came walking toward us. "Come on! We gotta move fast! This place is about to turn into a war zone!"

"What's going on?" Sheba asked.

"Orpheus is coming in with the Ortega cartel. They gave us a sweet deal to help them take the Moreno's out," Guap informed us. They were dropping bodies left and right as we hurried to the garage. We finally made it to the garage door, but Guap was hit in the chest. Sheba immediately fired her gun killing the guard that shot Guap. He fell to the floor. We kneeled down to help him get up.

"Get the fuck outta here. If you die, my death is meaningless," he said as his life began slipping from his body. Tears immediately started pouring from my eyes.

"I can't leave you here. You are my family, Guap," She cried as she tried to lift him. His life slipped away. She cried out in sorrow. "I can't leave his body here." She continued to try and lift him. We both used all the strength we had to lift him. We each threw one of his arms over our shoulders. We put his lifeless body in the trunk of the Mercedes. She rushed and retrieved the keys from the wall.

"I have no time to argue with you about this , Worth. Drive this car out of here. Don't stop until you feel safe. Take my phone. Go to the Casa Blanca Resort. Give them my name with the safe word *Dose Forever* and stay there until you hear from one of us."

"Where are you going?" I asked scared out of my mind.

"That's my brother and husband in there. I can't leave them. You have no choice. All this is for you. You have to walk away from this," she said as tears poured down her face. I hugged her as tight as I could. She rushed back into the house as I entered the car. I did as she said and sped out of the garage. Bullets immediately started flying at me. I screamed and ducked but never stopped. I realized the car was bulletproof. I drove as fast as I could. I kept checking the rearview mirror to see was I being followed. I never was. After realizing I was in the clear I pulled over to the side of the road. I cried until I couldn't cry anymore. I didn't know if I would ever see any of them again.

Fila

"I'll be back," I said to Paisley as I got out of bed.

"It's two o'clock in the morning. Where are you going?" She asked sitting up in the bed. I ignored her and continued getting dressed. She stopped me before I left the room.

"I know I can't stop you. Just please, be careful. Fiji needs you. Hell, I need you," she said with her beautiful soft eyes.

"I'll be safe. I ain't dying for another nigga to slide between them slim thighs," I said smiling. She giggled and smacked me on the arm.

I checked on Fiji before leaving the house. He was fast asleep in his bed. I needed to sit him down and discuss my relationship with Paisley. He thinks of Paisley as his friend. I needed for him to understand she will be more than a friend in his life. It reminded me of my plans for Estelle. Ma decided to stay at Pop's house. I dreaded the thought of attending his funeral in a couple of days. There was no way I could let the man that took his life continue to live on this earth. That cop will pay for killing my old man. Detective Bailey will suffer the consequences of bringing his self into my life. Estelle will pay the price for bringing them both into my life.

When I arrived at the hotel, I made my way to the back entrance. I made sure to stay away from all security cameras. I didn't want my presence here to be known. I pulled my hoodie over my head and headed up the flight of stairs. I entered the hotel room to see Detective Bailey tied to the bed. His ass was butt naked with his mouth gagged. Cora was sitting in a chair with sexy lingerie on smoking a blunt.

"Took you long enough," she said smiling at me.

"You know I was coming," I said taking the blunt from her. Cora is beautiful. She a thick, brown skinned dominatrix. When I first started hustling in the streets we connected. She was working the streets and hustling niggas. She tried robbing me but failed. I found her badly beaten one night in an alley. I started to leave her ass there but decided to help her. She started hustling the corners for me. She never left her previous life alone. She became smarter in the type of men she pursued. After she began offering Dominatrix sex, she started making more money than she could count.

"Your money will be in your account before noon,"
I told her.

"I'm never worried when it comes to your
payment," she said smiling at me. Her smile turned to a
frown. "I'm sorry about what happened to your father. He
was always so nice to me. He taught me a lot about these
mean ass streets." I nodded my head accepting her
sympathy.

"You bring what I needed?" I asked her. She
walked over to the dresser and retrieved the bag from her
purse.

"The pics will be uploaded soon as I get the call
from you," she said. I nodded my head. She had taken
compromising pictures of him that would ruin his
reputation.

I untied him. Cora left the room and I poured water
on Bailey to wake him up. He coughed as he sat up. He
tried getting out the bed until he heard my gun cock. He
froze and stared me in the eyes. "Nigga, you will pay for
this!"

I laughed. "You are in no position to be giving out
threats. I know you didn't think you would get away with
killing my old man."

"You will never get away with this. You will be the first one they suspect of killing me," he said staring at me.

"I'm not going to kill you," I said smiling. He looked at me curiously. There was a knock on the door. I walked over and opened the door. "Perfect timing," I said to Tree when he walked in with Officer Stone. He was the cop that fired the gun. His face was stressed. He looked at me with fear in his eyes.

"What the fuck is he doing here?" Detective Bailey said staring at him.

"He's here to do what needs to be done," I said smiling at him. He looked at me wanting to know more.

"It was an accident. I didn't mean to do it," Officer Stone pleaded with me.

"Man, shut the fuck up. We've already discussed this. You better do what needs to be done," Tree told him pointing the gun at his head.

"What's going on?" Bailey asked.

I walked over to the bed. "Since Officer Stone likes using his gun, we decided it's only right he be the one to handle you."

Detective Bailey laughed. "He would never jeopardize his career by killing me."

"You're right, but he wouldn't jeopardize his family for you either," Tree said giving Bailey a sinister smile. He looked at us with a confused expression.

"They're going to kill my wife and son. I don't have a choice," Stone said with water in his eyes. I had no sympathy for him. He let Bailey use him and now he has to pay the price.

"You stupid mothafucka. They aren't going to kill your family," Bailey spewed staring at Stone. Stone knew his family would be dead before he made it home if he didn't do as we said.

"Man, let's get this shit over with. I can't stay here looking at this pink booty redneck all night," Tree said rolling his eyes at Bailey.

I stared at Stone with a head nod. He pulled out his gun. His hand trembled as he pointed the gun at Bailey. I took the syringe and coke out the bag Cora gave me. "I'm going to make this easy for you. You're going to be so damn high you won't feel the bullets tearing through your flesh." I cooked the coke on a spoon turning it to liquid. I put it in the syringe. Bailey tried fighting me when I tried inserting it in his arm. Tree held him down covering his mouth with his hand. Tears started falling from his eyes. He felt his end coming.

"I told you I wasn't the nigga to fuck with," I said before shooting the hot liquid into his arm. He slumped immediately. His eyes were barely open.

I walked over to Stone. "Remove all your clothes." He looked at me to see if I was serious. Once he saw I was, he stripped naked. "You have two minutes to kill him or my partner here makes the call to have your family killed," I said glancing at Tree. Tree winked and held up his phone.

Stone started crying. I knew he felt like he wouldn't come out of this alive. He was right. He was a dead man just like Bailey. I looked to make sure the silencer was on the weapon. I didn't want gunshots echoing from the room. "Thirty seconds, white boy," Tree said.

Pow! Pow! Pow! Three shots entered Bailey's body. I could only assume anger took over Stone's mind and heart. He walked closer to the bed and put a hole in Bailey's head. He must've felt Bailey was the reason he was in this situation. His assessment was right. *You lay with dogs you get up with fleas.*

"Please, don't harm my family," he said with his head down.

"I am a man of my word." He held his gun to his head and splattered his brains all over Bailey's body.

"Clean whatever you touched in here. Let's get the fuck outta here," Tree said looking around. Killing Bailey and Stone wouldn't bring Pops back, but it made me feel better knowing they are dead. I wasn't going to let the system decide their fate. I've witnessed too many cops walk away from killing an innocent black man.

Basilio

I don't know what military wars are like, but drug wars are deadly and bloody. I didn't expect things to happen so fast. I thought I would have time to talk to Moreno. I needed to get answers about my mother and his father. Right now, my only concern was surviving the invasion from the Ortega family. We were on their side. The problem was I didn't know the Ortega family from the Moreno family. I was shooting my way through the house. I was looking for Dose. I wasn't going to leave my brother in this war zone. I turned the corner and was met by a gun in my face while I pointed mine in his face. Orpheus and I chuckled at each other and lowered our weapons.

"Damn, it's fucking Vietnam in this bitch. I've been killing and dodging niggas since I walked on this property," he said.

"Yeah, shit happened fast. I didn't think the Ortega's were coming this fast," I said looking over my shoulder.

"Shit, me neither. I received a call saying they were headed this way. I rushed here because I knew shit was getting ready to get crazy," he said. "I was lurking through the house looking for you. Come on, I got Moreno in the wine cellar." We could hear gunshots steadily being fired. We were on the west wing of the house. It was mostly empty. A few dead bodies were laid out on the floor as we made our way to the cellar.

"You haven't seen Dose?" I asked.

"Nah," he answered as he knocked on the cellar door. Moreno opened the door looking like a scared child. Orpheus locked the door behind us.

"I'm not saying shit until I have your word my life is safe," Moreno said pacing the floor.

"Mothafucka, I ain't promising you shit. I can kill you now. It's up to you if you want to take that chance," I warned him pointing the gun at his head. He started singing like a bird.

"My father knew he was dying. He wanted your father to take over the cartel to ensure our legacy would remain intact. He had no one to take his place. I didn't want it and Camila wasn't ready. Your father wanted out. He wanted to walk away from everything. He wanted his family to be free of this life. There was one obstacle in his way," he said staring at me.

"What?" I asked curiously. I didn't know my old man wanted out of this life. He never discussed his worries with me.

"Your mother. She didn't want out. She wasn't ready to lose the power they had. If your father stepped in my father's shoes, his power would be endless. Your mother lusted for the position they were offered," he continued.

"What are you saying?" I asked.

He stared at me with blank eyes. "Your mother made a deal with my father. She would remove your father and take the position he was offered."

My knees weakened. I couldn't believe what he was telling me. "You saying my mother killed my old man to run your father's cartel?"

He nodded his head in agreement. "God decided to bring karma to my father early for his sins and betrayal. He was diagnosed with an incurable cancer. This changed the rules of the game for your mother. As far as she was concerned, this was no longer our legacy. This was all hers.

She is the reason I would never let you out. It was always her decision to keep you here. She wants you to take over the cartel. The power she has is too much for her to give away. Father is so doped up he doesn't know what's going on. She's telling him one thing and doing something totally different. She never lets us visit him alone. She knows we will tell him."

I had no words for what he was telling me. It wasn't hard to believe. Everything he was saying made sense. It explains how she was still alive. Her death was staged. She was never harmed. She had risked our lives for years, so she could have control. The more I thought about it, the more enraged I became. She took our father away from us. He wanted the life for his family that I want with Worth. She won't win this time. If killing her is my only way out, her blood will be shed. I turned to walk away.

"What about him?" Orpheus asked.

I looked back at Moreno. I knew he would never be a threat to me. The sad part is he never was. "Let him go. If he makes it out the front gate without getting shot, he lives." I rushed out the cellar. Gun shots were at a minimum now. Orpheus was behind me as we made our way to the main house.

"I'm going to find Andre. He's the leader of the Ortega army. By the look of the bodies laying around, looks like the Moreno era is over," he said looking around.

"How the fuck can you tell one soldier from the other?" I asked looking at the bodies.

"The Ortega soldiers have red markings on their faces," he said. I looked down at the bodies. There were at least fifteen bodies. Only two had red markings on their faces. We went in different directions.

My heart dropped and my eyes filled with tears at what lay before me. My brother's bloody body laid on the floor. Dose has always been my right hand. He kept me sane when I felt overwhelmed. He was like my protector even when I didn't need to be protected. I never thought of him as anything less than family. I never imagined him not being in my life. We shared our dreams and goals together when we were young boys. We wanted to rule the drug empire. Our plans changed when the love for a woman filled our hearts. He married my twin sister. She's carrying his firstborn. He was so proud of becoming a father. I knew he would love and protect my sister with his life. Rage took over my heart when I looked up to see my mother cradling Sheba as she cried like a baby.

I raised my gun and pointed it at her. "Get yo fucking hands off her." Sheba immediately broke their embrace and turned to face me.

"Bull, what are you doing?" Sheba asked staring at me.

"Sheba, get over here," I demanded never taking my eyes off my mother.

"They killed him, Bull. He's gone," she cried more and kneeled down beside Dose's body. It broke my heart to hear the pain in her cry. I had to tell her the truth. I knew what I was going to say would only hurt her more.

"They didn't kill him. She did," I told her. Sheba looked up at me for answers. I stared at mother. "Tell your daughter you killed her husband and father of her child."

"I would never do anything to hurt Dose. He has always been like a son to me," she lied.

"Why would you say that, Bull?" She asked.

"She's been the mastermind behind everything. She staged her own death and killed our father. He wanted out, but she wanted more power. She made a deal with the Moreno cartel to take over since our father declined. She's the reason we couldn't walk away."

Sheba looked up at our mother. "Is this true?"

"Of course not. I guess you've been listening to Moreno's foolishness," she said nervously.

Sheba slowly stood up staring at her. "You did all this?"

She raised her gun and pointed it at Sheba. I almost pulled my trigger. If I did, Sheba would be dead too. "He didn't build this legacy on his own. I was there working side by side with him. He excluded me from making the decision to walk away or accept the offer. I deserved to have a say. We sacrificed so much to get where we were. I wasn't going to give all that up for a boring life. I'm more than a housewife. I have just as much knowledge to run an empire as any man. I wasn't going to turn down this opportunity and chance to prove it. I have some of the most powerful men in the world in my pockets. My power reaches the White House. No boring life could ever compare to what I have."

"You sacrificed a life with your children," Sheba said with tears running down her cheeks.

"I did this for us. All this is yours," she tried explaining.

"You will kill your own daughter for power and money?" I asked. I was fighting with all my strength not to pull the trigger.

"Hey, whatever this is you have to settle it some other place. This place is about to be swarming with all kinds of cops in a few," Orpheus said rushing into the room. He glanced at me and my mother pointing guns. Mine on her and hers on her daughter.

"I have to say goodbye to him," Sheba said kneeling down beside Dose. She sobbed and kissed his forehead gently. In one quick motion, she turned around and put a hole in our mother's head. I realized she kneeled down to retrieve Dose's gun.

"Fuck!" Orpheus barked as we both stood there shocked and speechless.

I walked over and eased the gun out of Sheba's hand. She stared down at our mother. "I'm sorry Bull. She wasn't the woman that loved and raised us. She sacrificed us for power and money."

"I know, Sis. We gotta get out of here," pulling her into my arms. She let out a gut-wrenching cry that shattered my heart.

"I'm not leaving his body here," she said once she stopped crying. Orpheus went over and lifted his body.

"Uuuuggghhh," Dose cried out in pain. Orpheus immediately dropped his body on the floor. We all stared down at him. "Fuck this shit hurts," he said snatching his shirt off.

Orpheus burst into laughter. "Nigga you got on a vest?"

"But all the blood?" She said staring at him. I chuckled, because I remembered what he would say about his vest.

"I had one made with blood bags in it. If I ever get hit, they'll assume I'm dead from all the blood leaking from me," he said. I could tell he was still in pain. Even though, he had on his vest the impact of the bullet alone can cause severe pain.

"Are you fucking serious? I thought you were dead?" She said charging and beating him in the chest. I laughed with joy. My brother was still alive.

"I'm sorry. Shit, I was knocked out fucking cold. The bitch shot me about five damn times. She was trying to kill my black ass for real," Dose said holding Sheba's arms.

"We gotta get out of here," I said. We rushed out of the house.

Once we were in a car leaving the mansion. I realized Worth wasn't with Sheba. Sheba was supposed to leave with her. "Where is Worth?"

"I sent her to the hotel. I couldn't leave you and him here. It's been us since day one. I made sure she was safe first, Bull."

Dose filled us in on what happened with our mother. He heard her over the phone ordering Moreno to be killed when all the chaos broke out. After he confronted her, she confessed to being behind everything. She gave him a bullshit sob story about being blackmailed with our lives. The moment she caught him off guard she tried to kill him. All I wanted now was to see Worth. I wasn't going to relax until I saw for myself that she was safe. I thought about my father as we drove. He didn't make it out to enjoy life. I'm going to make sure I live a carefree enough life for the both of us. I felt no remorse for our mother. She betrayed and killed a man that loved her with his soul.

Worth

It's been hours since I arrived at the hotel. I couldn't eat or sleep. I didn't know if everyone was dead or alive. Here I was in a strange country where I knew no one. There's a dead body in the car that Sheba left me with. I didn't know who I could trust for help. All of a sudden, I remembered the password Sheba gave me. I decided to go downstairs to ask someone for help. I needed to get back to the mansion to see if anyone was still alive. I couldn't leave not knowing if they were alive or dead. I became sick to my stomach when I thought of the possibility of Basilio's demise. If he was dead, everything we went through would be pointless. I grabbed my keys from the nightstand and the gun I took from Guap's body. When I opened the door, my heart felt as if it was going to burst.

"Where you going?" Basilio asked staring at me.

"To find y'all," I said staring at him with watery eyes. I was so overjoyed to see him I couldn't hold back the tears. He walked in the room and closed the door.

"Bella, what have I told you about carrying a gun?" He said taking the gun from my hand.

Natavia Presents

I wrapped my arms around him burying my face into his neck. I sobbed as he held me tight. "I was so scared. I thought you were dead."

"I'm good, Bella. We're good," he whispered in my ear. I realized Sheba and Dose wasn't with him.

"Where are Sheba and Dose?" I asked breaking our embrace.

"They checked into a room. Everyone is okay," he assured me.

"I'm sorry. Guap was killed trying to save us. His body is in the trunk. That's his gun. What are we going to do with his body? We can't take him home with us," I rambled.

"We'll give him a proper burial here. Only family he had was us," he told me. That broke my heart even more.

I remembered Basilio's mother. "Your mother?" The look in his eyes told it all. I could see the pain in them. Regardless of her actions, she was the woman that birthed and once loved him. "I'm sorry."

"Bella, you have nothing to be sorry for. She did all this. All you ever did was love me," he said staring at me.

"Is it over?" I asked.

Natavia Presents

"It's over. I still have to make sure business is still flowing, but we are free," he said. I couldn't help a smile from appearing on my face. We could finally have the life we fought so hard for.

He sat his and Guap's gun on the nightstand. He pulled his shirt over his head and removed the bulletproof vest. I licked my lips as I stared at his muscular torso. "I'm going to take a shower. Someone will be bringing some clothes by in a couple of hours."

"What about Guap's body? We can't just leave it in the trunk."

"It's already being handled. We'll have a small service for him before we leave tomorrow," he assured me.

He went into the bathroom to shower. I sat on the edge of the bed thanking God for bringing him back to me. I had already taken a shower, but I decided to join him. I wanted to feel his flesh against mine. My pussy throbbed at the thought of him sliding inside me. I removed my clothes and entered the bathroom. I eased the shower door open to see him sitting on the bench. His eyes were closed while his head leaned against the wall. The sprayers wet my hair and body as I walked toward him. I kneeled between his legs waking him up. He looked down at me as I wrapped my hand around his dick. It immediately started to harden. His stiff rod jumped in my hand when my tongue stroked the head. I licked and slurped more and more into my mouth. My saliva spilled out down his shaft as I enjoyed sliding him deeper inside my mouth. I could hear soft groans coming from him as I licked and slurped up and down his hard dick. The thick veins in his shaft were like bolts of lightning. I used both my hands to massage him while my wet mouth continued to suction him inside my mouth.

"Damn! Bella!" He barked gripping a handful of my hair. Hearing the satisfaction in his voice made me want more of him. Faster, deeper and nastier I sucked him as saliva poured out my mouth. I could feel his dome hitting my throat. I used one of my hands to fondle his full balls. I continued slobbing and sucking until he couldn't take it any longer. "Aaaarrrrggghhhh!" He roared unloading inside my mouth. His body jerked and trembled as I gulped down every drop.

He massaged my scalp through my hair until I satisfied my taste buds with his flavor. I stood up and he turned me around so my back was facing him. He gently pushed down on my back bending me over. He spread my legs apart and slid two fingers between my wet, slippery slit. My knees buckled when I felt his long thick tongue lapping back and forth between my lips. He licked and sucked my juices as they poured from me. His strong hands massaged my ass cheeks as he feasted on my pussy. His tongue caressed my swollen clit causing me to cry out in pleasure. I cried out in ecstasy when he spread my ass cheeks and twirled his tongue around my ass. He finger fucked my dripping wet tunnel while his tongue lapped between my cheeks.

"Oh God! Yes! Please don't stop!" He became a starved animal feasting on me. "Oooooohhhh! I'm cccooomming!" I cried out as my body stiffened and quivered. He grunted loudly as he licked and sucked my creamy center. I couldn't hold myself up any longer. He grabbed me around my waist and sat me in his lap with my back to him before I fell. He wasn't done with me. He lifted me up and slid his brick hard dick inside me.

"Mierda este cono caliente y mojado!" *Shit this pussy hot and wet* he whispered in my ear as he bounced me up and down his shaft. My wet ass slapped against his wet body as I enjoyed pleasure and pain. He licked, sucked and bit my back and neck as I started bouncing with his help. He reached around and started massaging my throbbing clit.

"Oh God! Yes!" I screamed as I slid up and down his pole. I could feel his dick spreading inside me.

"Muy apretado *So tight*," he said as I felt myself getting ready to explode. My walls gripped his shaft as my mouth watered and legs trembled.

"Aaaaahhhh! Yyyyeeesss!!" I wailed as a loud barbaric roar erupted from his gut. Our bodies jerked and shook as we released our essence on each other.

"Tu eres mi alma *You are my soul*," he whispered in my ear as I relaxed against his chest.

I stood up and straddled his lap. I loved him with my soul. I placed his hand on my baby bump. "You are my life."

Paisley

I couldn't believe what I was hearing on the news. I sat watching with my mouth wide open. I don't know how, but I knew Fila has something to do with this. I felt a sense of vindication. Bailey deserved what happened to him. Stone was equally responsible for pulling the trigger. The news reporter said Bailey and Stone were found dead in a hotel room. There was drugs on the scene. Stone left a letter apologizing for his actions. The letter stated he was having a sexual relationship with Bailey. He followed Bailey to the hotel and discovered he was meeting a woman there. In the letter, he went on to say that after the woman left he entered the room. He and Bailey argued before he lost control and killed him. Unable to handle the consequences of his actions, he turned the gun on himself. The letter stated how he and Bailey were using high school kids to push drugs for them. He also stated they planted evidence and blackmailed suspects in many cases.

"Well, karma is a mothafucka," Veronica said smiling at the television. I smiled at her. Fila and Fiji came walking into the den. He had taken Fiji out for breakfast. Fiji walked over to me with a big smile on his face.

"You gone be my other mommy. I gotta think of something to call you. Daddy said it's not respectful to call you Paisley. Ms. Paisley makes you sound old. You ain't old like G-Ma," he said. Fila burst into laughter. I covered my mouth to keep from laughing.

"Boy, I'm gone whoop yo ass. I'm not damn old," she said bopping her head. Fiji giggled and jumped in my lap.

I know! I got G-Ma. You can be P-Ma," he said smiling at me. I didn't care what he called me as long as he was willing to give me a chance. I looked up at Fila. He winked at me as he smiled.

"Come on, let's go get your bag," Veronica said standing up. Yesterday was Carl's funeral. Veronica was taking Fiji to New York with her for a week. When they left the room, he came and sat beside me on the couch.

"He told me I was slow. He said he knew you was my girlfriend. He knew it meant you was like another mama to him. His friend got another mama. He can't wait to tell him it's official that you his other mama." I laughed.

"I just saw the news. How are you?" I asked in a low voice.

"It doesn't bring him back, but I feel vindicated. I've made my peace with losing him. We've talked," he said winking at me. "All I have to do now is continue making him proud."

"Did he tell you to make sure you shampoo and grease my scalp once a week?" I asked smiling at him.

He laughed and stood up. "Nah, but I gotcha as long as that pussy keeps gripping my dick."

I laughed. "You so nasty."

"You like it. Come on, take a ride with me," he said pulling me off the couch.

"Where? They are leaving in a few hours. I want to say goodbye," I reminded him.

"We'll be back in plenty of time," he said.

Once I realized where we were going, I looked at him like he was crazy. We didn't need to be nowhere near a police station. "Why are we here?" I asked as he parked.

"You'll see," he said winking at me. He told me to sit in the waiting area before he walked to the front desk. A few minutes later, a plain clothes cop walked up to him. They talked for a few minutes.

"Come on," he said walking over to me. I didn't know what was going on, but I definitely wanted to know. I followed behind him. We walked down a long hall until we came to a room. The cop unlocked the door. It was an interrogation room. A table and chairs were the only things in the room. There was also a two-way mirror. We sat in the two chairs that sat on one side of the table. My heart started beating fast. I prayed no one discovered any information that would bring criminal charges on Fila.

"What's going on?" I asked Fila scared to hear the answer. The door opened before he could respond. I was beyond shocked to see Estelle walk in the room in handcuffs. I stared at Fila for answers. Estelle sat across from us. Her eyes were red and swollen. She was in an orange jumpsuit and handcuffs. She looked at Fila pleading for help without speaking a word.

"You did this?" She asked as she started to cry.

He smiled at her and slid some papers over to her. "You have two choices. You can sit in prison for years or you can sign over custody of Fiji to me and walk out a free woman."

"I won't let this bitch raise my son," she spewed with anger. I decided to sit in silence.

"Either way, I will win. You think they will give him to a mother fighting federal drug charges. The phone you tried blackmailing Paisley with, it'll be logged as evidence against you. Those are conspiracy and murder charges."

"You can't do that!" She screamed with anger.

"You're right. I can't. The same way you used the system against me, I decided to return the favor. I'll let them do my dirty work. You were warned," he said. She cried harder because she knew she didn't have a choice. She angrily signed the papers and threw them in his face.

"I will allow you to have supervised visits with him one day out the weekend. I would advise you to get a job, because my money won't support you and your family any longer."

"You won't get away with this. I know you put those drugs in my car," she cried.

"I don't sell drugs. I'm a legit business man," Fila said standing up winking his eye at her. I stood up with him. She screamed her hate for him and me as we left the room.

"Remind me never to fuck with you the wrong way," I said as we sat in the car.

He laughed. "We got one more stop to make. Then we can go home."

"How do you think Fiji is going to handle only seeing his mother once a week?" I asked him.

"I talked with him. I explained she's going to be working a lot. If I see a change in her attitude, I'll negotiate with her on her visitation. As for now, I'm doing what's best for him." I nodded my head in agreement. We pulled into the parking lot of an empty building. It was a building I was considering leasing for my shop. We exited the car and walked to the door.

"Here," he said handing me a set of keys. My eyes grew big as I stared at him.

"You didn't?" I asked.

"Open the door, P-Ma," he said smiling. I laughed.

"Surprise!" Everyone screamed startling me when I opened the door.

"Oh my God!" I said covering my mouth. I couldn't believe everyone was here. I didn't even know Worth and everyone was back home.

"We tricked you P-Ma," Fiji said excited.

"Yes, you did," I said lifting him up.

"I thought we talked about you picking me up like a baby," he said. Everyone laughed.

"You're right. I'm sorry," I said putting him down. I looked around the room at everyone. It warmed my heart to see my friends and family. Even Nika was here with Tree. It seemed they are the perfect fit for each other. She was finally getting her life together. The biggest shocker was when Mama came walking up to me. I didn't know what to expect.

Natavia Presents

"Congratulations baby, I'm so proud of you," she said pulling me into a tight hug. "I'm sorry for all the animosity I've held onto for years."

"It's okay Mama. I'm so happy you are here." I hugged her tighter.

She broke our embrace. "Well, I didn't have a choice. A handsome, young gentleman came to my doorstep confessing his love for you. Then he had the audacity to read me." She winked at Fila who was standing behind me. I looked around the room at everyone. Everyone looked so happy. This was perfect. Mama walked away talking with Worth's mom. Fila was in a corner talking to Bull, Dose and Tree. Worth came walking toward me with a big smile on her face.

"You are really starting to show," I said smiling at her.

"I know," she said rubbing her little belly. "You see our mother's are bonding. They're going on a cruise in a couple of weeks. I'm happy to see them enjoying their lives again."

"I've never seen my mom smile so much. I remember she couldn't stand to be in the same room with my dad. How's your dad doing?" I asked her.

"He's recovering well. He's mad because Mommy is going on a cruise. She says she having too much fun to settle down," I said laughing.

"His loss," I shrugged my shoulders.

"It is. I can't feel sorry for him. He brought this on himself. Once he makes a full recovery, I'm sure he'll be back to doing him."

"Probably so. I didn't know you were coming back this way. You said you were going to travel with Bull before coming home," I told her.

"I couldn't miss your surprise. Besides, he has to handle some business before we go. We're going to travel so many places. I can't wait. We plan on leaving next week," she said excitedly.

"Well, at least Sheba will be here to help me design and decorate this place. I gotta pick out a designer."

"You know she'll be happy to do it."

"Never imagined our lives would turn out this way. I didn't think it was going to happen some times. It felt like everything was against us," Worth said looking at Bull. She was truly in love, like I was with Fila.

"Now that we have the life we want. Let's enjoy it."

We did. We all danced, talked and laughed until we were exhausted.

Natavia Presents

Epilogue

1 year later

Worth

Life couldn't be better. We traveled to so many different countries. My favorite was Brazil, because he proposed to me there. When he asked me, I accepted and didn't want to wait. He made it happen. He flew everyone there to attend our wedding. I became his wife in Brazil. We traveled for four months before returning home. Basilio made sure I visited doctors to check up on our life growing inside me. I was seven months pregnant when we returned home. Two months later I gave birth to our son. Basilio wanted to continue his father's name, so his name is Basilio Artez Vega III. Sheba gave birth a month before me. She had a son also. He was named after Dose making him a Junior. Love was attending NYU pursuing her dream. My dad has fully recovered. He's still trying to win Mommy back, but she's dating and loving life. She and Paisley's mom have become great friends. They stay going on cruises and road trips. Paisley is busy running her salon. Business was so good, she had to hire a second stylist to help her out some days. Fila is still handling business on a much higher level.

As for me, I'm still adjusting to motherhood. I've started putting in applications to manage a hotel. I didn't go to school all those years just to have a degree. I plan to put it to use. Basilio wanted me to wait a few years before I started working. I wasn't waiting that long. I plan to be working before our son turns one.

"What we doing here? I need to get home to breastfeed," I said rolling my eyes. I never planned on breastfeeding. Basilio was adamant about me doing it. I gave in eventually. I don't regret breastfeeding, but I didn't want him to know I like doing it.

"I just wanted you to see your place of employment," he said smiling at me.

"What?" I asked confused.

"This is my hotel I'm having built. You will manage it. Just because you're my wife, don't think I'm not going to stay in your ass about my business."

I jumped up and down excitedly. "Oh my God! Thank you! I love you! I promise you won't regret it! When will it open?"

"In a few months," he replied. I reached over hugging him tight with a big, sloppy wet kiss.

"I promise. I won't disappoint you," I said smiling.

"I know you won't," he said winking at me.

"My soul, my life," I said.

"Dos corazones alma *Two hearts one soul*," he said kissing my lips softly.

Everything we endured was worth the happiness and love we feel now.

The End

Natavia Presents

To stay updated on Nona Day's releases follow her on:

https://www.amazon.com/-/e/B06X92PRMZ

https://www.facebook.com/groups/137785320163038/?re

f=bookmarks

https://www.facebook.com/nonadaynovels/

A Love Worth the Fight 3   Nona Day

CPSIA information can be obtained
at www.ICGtesting.com
Printed in the USA
LVHW051514030919
629788LV00011B/870/P